CAPE MAY SUMMER NIGHTS

CLAUDIA VANCE

CHAPTER ONE

With moving boxes stacked heavy and full in her arms, Margaret stopped in front of Dave's beach house to watch some beachgoers cross the street with their carts and chairs. She smiled at how delighted and excited they seemed to spend a day on the bay beach. As she stood there taking in the moment, she realized sweat poured off her face. It was the end of the June, and the weather was getting hotter and hotter by the day.

Suddenly, Dave walked out of the house and caught her attention. "Hey, you. Whatcha daydreaming about?"

Margaret snapped out of it while shifting the boxes she held. "Oh, I was just admiring the happy families walking to the beach. It's such a great place to live."

Dave smiled, gratefully grabbing the boxes from her before making his way back towards the house. "I have to say, I'm loving the idea of moving in here more and more. I think I made the right choice."

Margaret paused to take a deep breath and blot the sweat from her face as Chris's truck pulled into the driveway next door, the back piled high with furniture and moving boxes.

Sarah jumped out of the truck, bursting with excitement and happiness. "Today is the day! Can you believe it?"

Margaret laughed. "How funny that both you and Dave are moving in on the same day."

Sarah smiled while looking across the street at the sunny beach. "Totally. I can't believe I get to live across the street from this view and with this hunk of a man."

Chris chuckled while blushing, waved hello to Margaret, then jumped into the back of the truck to maneuver the furniture, before handing a couple of boxes to Sarah.

Dave came back outside holding two mason jars full of water with fresh-squeezed lemon. He handed one to Margaret before noticing Chris and Sarah. "Hey there, neighbors! Looks like we've all got our work cut out for us today, eh?"

Sarah peered over the boxes piled high in her arms "Can you believe I was able to get out of my rental so soon? My lease required a sixty-day notice, but as it turns out, my landlord decided to put the place on the market and wanted to get in and make changes. We agreed on July 1 as my last day, but I'm moving in a few days early because why not?"

Dave nodded while looking towards Margaret. "It worked out nicely, didn't it? Well, I'm heading back inside. I'll catch up with you guys later. Let me know if you need anything."

Chris jumped out of the back of his truck. "Same. Let us know if you need help with anything."

After Dave went back inside, Margaret hoisted herself into the back of his truck, trying to find something else to bring inside. She stopped to look back over at Sarah and Chris, who seemed like the happiest people on the planet. They were giggling, smiling, and playfully nudging each other as they walked in and out of the house carrying different items. They seemed like two teenagers in love for the first time, even briefly dancing with each other in the grass before unloading the next boxes.

Margaret's heart sank a little. She was happy for Sarah and

Chris, but a part of her wished Dave, herself, and the girls were moving in together, even if the idea of it wasn't exactly practical. She already had a wonderful home with a beautiful yard and garden, but she still felt envious. Her relationship with Dave seemed to be moving at a snail's pace compared to Sarah and Chris's.

Just then, a car pulled up behind Dave's truck in the driveway.

Margaret looked over to see her mother, Judy, stepping out with a bag. "Hi, Mom. Decided to stop by and help?"

Judy shook her head and laughed. "Oh, no. Not feeling up to that today, but I did make you two some lunch. It's all in this bag here. I hope you're hungry."

Margaret jumped down from the bed of the truck, gave her mom a hug, and took the bag. "Definitely. I think we're just about ready to take a lunch a break. Thank you, Mom."

Judy looked at her watch. "Well, I hope you enjoy it. I have to jet off and meet your dad. By the way, you haven't forgotten about our annual Fourth of July week with family this year? They should be here by the second."

Margaret chuckled. "No, Mom. I haven't forgotten. I guess they really liked spending the holiday in Cape May last year, so they wanted to come again, eh?"

Judy smiled. "Yep. It's too bad the Seahorse is fully booked and can't accommodate them like last year. It's looking like your cousins from Arizona have decided to come this year, and we're getting low on space to put them up. I've got a full house, and so does Liz with family staying over. Do you have any more room at your place?"

Margaret thought for a moment. "Well, I already have the girls bunking with me in my room. I'm not sure I have much more space unless…"

Just then, Dave walked outside, overhearing the conversation. "Judy! You're here at last. We were waiting for the real help to arrive and save us."

Judy laughed. "Very funny. I brought you two lunch, though, so that's something."

Dave peered in the bag and inhaled the yummy aromas. "It smells amazing. So, what's this I hear about not having enough room, if you don't mind me prying?"

Margaret sighed. "Just family stuff. We have more cousins coming in from Arizona who have decided last minute to join our Fourth of July family week. And there isn't anywhere to put them up; you know how everything is booked up in Cape May right now."

Dave scratched his chin and smiled at Margaret. "Easy. You and the girls stay with me here, and let your family stay at your place. Will that give them enough room?"

Margaret's heart fluttered a little as she tried to subdue her excitement. "Well, yeah. I think that could work for my cousins, but will it work for you?"

Dave turned his hat backwards on his head, his thick salt-and-pepper hair shining in the sunlight, a twinkle appearing in his blue eyes. "Of course."

Judy smiled and winked at Dave. "Sounds like we have a plan, then, eh?"

* * *

Meanwhile across Cape May, Liz and Donna walked around town together after grabbing lunch.

Liz took a sip of her iced coffee and looked down the street. "I could be wrong, but I heard there's a funky new hotel that way that just opened. Would you want to go scope it out with me?"

Donna dropped her sunglasses over her eyes and took a sip of her iced tea. "You bet. Let's do it."

Once at the hotel, they noticed the tiny, barely legible sign out front with the name The Sand Pit.

"Interesting name," Liz said with a little skepticism as she stared up at the sign.

They walked through the front doors into what looked like a still unfinished hotel. The lobby walls were stark white and there was very little of anything anywhere. No furniture. No help desk. Not even a single thing hanging on any wall.

Donna pushed her sunglasses down on her nose. "Well, apparently, they are *not* open yet, and this is anything but funky. There's nothing and nobody here."

Liz shrugged. As they started to make their way back out of the front doors, a man came bounding out of nowhere.

"Can I help you?" he asked frantically, making his way towards a delivery driver who had appeared behind them.

Liz and Donna abruptly turned around. "Oh, we're sorry. We just wanted to see the new hotel, but it appears you aren't open yet," Donna said.

The man chuckled while signing for the packages and looked back at Liz and Donna. "I'll have you know that we *are* indeed open. What makes you think we aren't?"

Liz chimed in. "Well, I'm an interior designer, and I wanted to see what you did with the place, but there's nothing here. Where's all of the furniture? Where's the staff? It surely doesn't look open."

The man laughed, as though dismissing the fact that Liz was an interior designer. "I'll have you know that I hired an interior designer. Melody told me the minimalistic approach is in. So, that's what we went for. That's why you don't see furniture. I can't keep up on the newest trends, which is why I hired someone young and enthusiastic. Someone more in touch with what's in with the younger generations."

Donna furrowed her brow. "Are the younger generations the only ones you're marketing to here?"

That man thought for a moment. "Well, no. But this minimalist decor is sure nice on the wallet, if you know what I'm saying."

Liz shrugged before turning back towards the doors. "Well, we wish you luck."

The man squinted his eyes. "You think you can do better? I challenge you to tell me right now what you would do different with this space."

Donna eyes widened as she waited for what Liz would say.

Liz turned around slowly, taking a last long, loud sip of her drink, then methodically paced around the room, eyeing every nook and cranny from floor to ceiling for five minutes.

She stopped in front of the man as he waited patiently for her. "Well, you need pops of color to give more warmth to this room if you're going to have white walls. It feels like a doctor's office with this fluorescent lighting, so that has to go. I would probably add some shabby chic hanging light fixtures with warm lighting. How about some plants? These concrete floors make the room feel so unfinished, I'd install dark wood flooring. Now, you can still be a minimalistic by getting a smaller help desk, but you'll need *something* for check in and check out. I would also add a sitting area with couches, chairs, and chaises. Also, there's not enough sunlight in here. Why are all the windows barricaded with dark blinds? These are things that draw people in. I don't work with hotel clients, but I do know this from past research. There's a method to how things are designed and decorated that speak to the customer."

The man raised his eyebrows. "I'm impressed."

Liz smiled. "I do this for a living. I know what I'm talking about. May I ask why the hotel is called The Sand Pit?"

The man smiled. "Come with me. I'll show you."

Donna and Liz, now giddy at how the day had evolved, followed him outside and through a gate into a large fenced area not seen from the road.

Liz and Donna's mouths dropped open. There, behind the fence, was golden sand—everywhere. It looked like a beach had been dropped right there in front of them. On the sand were many tables and chairs with umbrellas and a large tiki bar.

Donna pushed her sunglasses down the bridge of her nose again to take a better look. "Well, I was *not* expecting *this* at all. This is everything."

The man smiled with pride. "Well, as you can see this is where the name came from. We couldn't get a spot on the beach for the hotel, so I brought the beach to us."

Liz walked over to the tiki bar and sat on one of the stools, looking around at the emptiness inside. "Where are the bartenders?"

The man sat next to Liz on the other stool. "Well, that is the one thing that's not open yet. We are still working out the details of the outside portion."

Liz looked around the beachy area, falling more in love with it the more she sat there. "You know. I'd like to add a couple things to my challenge. You need some super-cool beach or tiki inspired paintings around your hotel. I would also jazz up your tiny sign out front. Make it bigger, for one. There is so much personality in this place, and I think you need to home in on that with your design."

The man smiled and held out his hand. "I'm Fred, and you are?"

Liz shook his hand. "I'm Liz, and this my friend Donna."

Donna put her arm around Liz's shoulders as she shook Fred's hand. "So, are you giving my friend here a job?"

Liz laughed. "Like I need another job. It was fun to be put up to the challenge, though. We have to get going, but I look forward to stopping over for some tiki drinks when your beach opens."

Donna and Liz said goodbye and headed out the gate.

Fred rubbed his chin in thought, before calling out towards Liz, "How much?"

Liz peered over the fence they now stood on the other side of. "For what?"

"For you to completely redesign my entire place?" Fred asked curiously.

Liz shrugged. "I don't know. I haven't seen the entire place. Not to mention, I don't normally work for hotel clients, and I'm currently taking the summer off."

Fred pulled out a piece of paper, scribbled something on it, and slipped it over the fence. "How's this number look for a month's worth of work?"

Liz opened the piece of paper, and her mouth dropped in shock.

Donna nudged Liz, silently mouthing, "Is he for real?"

Liz shrugged but felt excitement building inside of her. That paycheck would be equal to six months of her normal work. "Well, for a month, I think we can maybe work something out. I work alone, though—unless it's someone I know. Just a warning. Also, I'm hosting some family coming in on the second for the Fourth of July week, so I don't think I'll be able to start until after that."

Fred did a hop of happiness behind the fence and walked around to meet them on the other side, holding his hand out for a shake. "That's fine. So, we have a deal?"

Liz gave a half-smile while shaking her head at Donna, who seemed to be over the moon. "It seems so."

CHAPTER TWO

The next day, Judy and Bob had decided to do a little afternoon shopping together when Bob got hung up in the camping section.

"Judy. Come here for a second," Bob said eagerly.

Judy stopped browsing the different varieties of yoga mats and followed Bob's voice to the next aisle. "OK, I'm here, Bob."

Bob pointed to a tent for sale. "Look at this. Isn't it great?"

Judy laughed. "It's huge. That's for a family of ten. What are you going to do with it?"

Bob stared in awe at the tent. "Camp, of course. I haven't camped since I was a kid. My family used to go on camping vacations every year. It just makes me feel all warm and fuzzy thinking about it."

Judy's eyes widened. "Who exactly are you going to camp with? I'm surely not—"

Bob interrupted her. "You, of course, and anyone else that wants to join."

Judy sighed. "I don't know about this, Bob. You know this was never a tradition in my family. We were always more indoorsy, I guess you could say," she said with a chuckle.

Bob grabbed a camping stove sitting nearby the tents. "Just think of the fun meals we can cook on this out under the stars, surrounded by tall trees and a fire. Doesn't it just make your heart leap?"

Judy laughed while leaning over to grab a camping set of wine glasses. "Well, this looks more my speed to be honest."

Bob looked back at the tent, then to Judy. "Well, what do you say? Should I buy it?"

Judy rolled her eyes. "Bob, you know this isn't my thing. We'll be lying on the ground, which I'm sure won't be a wonderful night's sleep. Then, where will I use the bathroom and shower? You know I have to pee a million times throughout the night. Am I going to wander out into the darkness with the bears while you're snoring away in the tent? And what about the bugs? They'll be invited into our tent every time we open it."

Bob put his hand on Judy's shoulder. "You worry too much. The joy of camping comes with the stress-free, relaxing environment of nature that you're put in. No laptops. No TV. The pressure of a schedule and home duties are gone. You get quality time with your loved ones and friends like you don't get at other places. It's really a unique experience, and I miss it so."

Judy put her hand on her hip, a small smile appearing on her face. "Fine. But we're getting this deluxe air mattress to put in the tent."

Bob clapped his hands in happiness. "Oh, you bet! I'm filling this cart up with all of the camping goodies."

Judy chuckled. "Well, don't go too crazy. Do you even know where you'd want our first camping adventure to take place?"

Bob stopped putting things in his cart to think for a moment. "Well, actually I did have one place in mind. Assateague Island. You know, where those wild horses are? Over by Ocean City, Maryland? I figure I can get in some nice fishing too."

Judy furrowed her brow. "Oh yeah, the *other* Ocean City. Well, it'll have to happen after our family leaves town."

Bob nodded and went back to happily eyeing every piece of camping equipment for sale.

* * *

Dale hopped in his car and before driving away, called Greg.

"Hey, Dale," Greg said when he answered the phone.

"Greg. Last minute, but what are you up to right now?"

Greg looked around his restaurant, everything was sparkling clean and perfectly set up. In the kitchen, chefs Mike and Ron and the kitchen team prepped food. "Well, just getting ready for the soft opening tonight. You're still coming, right?"

Dale nodded. "Most definitely. Do you think you're all set and ready?"

Greg looked over at his chefs, who happily nodded back at him. "I think so."

Dale buckled his seat belt. "Great. Well, do you have an hour to spare to come look at something with me in Wildwood? I really could use another opinion."

Greg hesitated, there may have been more to do for the soft opening but ultimately, he decided there really wasn't. "Sure. A nice break before the big night might be good."

"Perfect. I'll pick you up in thirty minutes," Dale said before hanging up the phone and shifting the car into drive.

Thirty minutes later, Dale waited in his car for Greg.

Greg hopped in. "You sure you don't want to come in and have a look at the restaurant before tonight?"

Dale put the car into drive. "Nah, I want to be surprised. Anyway, I was helping my buddy in Ocean City today, and I got the call about an opportunity over in Wildwood. I definitely need your input. Thank you for this last-minute favor."

Greg leaned back in the car's seat as Dale turned up the radio when an old favorite reggae song started to play.

Twenty minutes later, they pulled up to a parking spot right off of the Wildwood Boardwalk, which bustled with people.

Greg furrowed his brow. "The boardwalk, eh? This is where the opportunity is?"

Dale laughed. "Yep, and wait till you see what it is."

After a quarter mile of walking the wide wooden boardwalk, crowded with people and full of many noises and yummy fried food smells, they arrived to a little area of food carts where people stood in long lines.

Dale opened his arms to the food cart area. "This is it. This is the opportunity."

Greg laughed. "Uh, what exactly are you talking about? I see nothing but food carts."

Dale pointed to his head, signifying a light bulb going on. "That's it! I think I'm putting a food cart here. I did some research, and some of these make a killing. Just look at these long lines."

Greg shifted his eyes left to right. "Isn't that a lot to take on for someone running their own restaurant and who lives over an hour away?"

Dale shrugged his shoulders. "Well, some of that may be changing, but I don't feel like getting into it right now. What do you think, though?"

Greg walked over to one of the food carts, nodded politely to the owners and peered in for a look-see. He noticed customers ordering different kinds of corn on the cobs. Some were smothered in a butter basil sauce, some were the elote corn—a Mexican street corn with mayonnaise, chili powder, cotija cheese, and a squeeze of lime. Another person ordered one cob with a cinnamon-sugar butter topping.

Dale smiled. "Who knew corn on the cob could be made so many different ways. I don't plan on doing corn on the cob, of course."

Greg looked around the crowded boardwalk, then back at Dale. "So, what is your plan then?"

Dale pointed to a large sign to the right. "Funnel cakes. And not just regular ole funnel cakes. Gourmet funnel cakes with homemade toppings. Not that apple pie filling glop from a can that the other places use here on the boardwalk. It will be exponentially better, and there will be some surprising flavors that I think will tantalize anyone's tastebuds."

Greg nodded, feeling thoroughly impressed. "OK, I'm liking your idea. I think you're onto something here. But do you have a cart? Do you have someone to man the cart?"

Dale got in line for a cob of corn. "I have connections. I think it will work out nicely. I'm hoping it get it off the ground within a week or so. Enough time to take advantage of the summer business."

Greg took a long breath of the salt air. "This location is great. The boardwalk, the beach. You can't lose. If you think it will work for you, then I say go for it."

Dale put his hand up for a high five. "Awesome. Grab a corn on the cob with me. Let's grub before we head back, I'm excited for your soft opening tonight."

Just then, a volley ball came hurtling towards Greg's head as he stood next to Dale in the back of the line.

Thump. Greg caught the ball, then looked around the boardwalk to see where it had come from.

Dale stared at him in astonishment. "How? Where? You must have super-powerful instinctive reflexes. You caught that like you knew it was coming."

Greg laughed while palming the volleyball and looking around the boardwalk "Funny enough, I grew up with a volleyball net in the backyard. I'd have the whole neighborhood and part of my class over just about every other night for volleyball games. It's one of my fondest memories from back then. I guess it's stuck with me, though I haven't played in years."

A couple of guys came running towards Greg from the beach. "Oh, thank you so much. Did we hit you with that?"

Greg smiled proudly. "Nope, I caught it. I used to play for years."

One of the guy's eyes widened. "Really? We are desperate for players. Why don't you join our league.?"

Greg shook his head. "I'm sorry guys, I'm just about to open a restaurant and have barely a lick of free time."

Dale furrowed his brow. "Just do it. I'm sure you can make it work. I think it'll be good for you. It's summer after all."

Greg released a deep sigh then looked back at the guys. "Just what my wife needs—me being home less, but let me talk it over with her. Give me your number in the meantime."

"Perfect. I'm Pete and this is Brian. We just had a couple guys bail. Why don't you join too?" Pete asked Dale, who wasn't paying much attention to the conversation anymore.

"Me?" Dale asked with a surprised laugh. "I have never played volleyball except those few times we had to during gym class."

After Pete gave his number to Greg, he looked back over at Dale. "We play every Tuesday night. We alternate between this beach and Cape May. Just show up. It'll be fun, I promise," he said, then he and Brian turned to make their way back to the beach.

Dale shook his head with a smile. "How do I always get myself into these things, Greg?"

Greg laughed. "Uh, I think you mean *we*."

* * *

That evening, Some of Greg's family and friends arrived to Heirloom's soft opening. It was a private event with an exclusive guest list before the grand opening to the public.

The restaurant was set up beautifully both inside and

outside, but because the weather was so perfect, all of the table seating had been arranged on the grand front porch.

Liz and the boys were the first to arrive. She held her hand to her mouth and gasped at the beauty when they stepped out of the car and onto the sidewalk out front.

White tied-back drapes were swathed around the porch, creating an elegant, whimsical feel. Each table had tea lights and large bouquets of purple hydrangeas that matched the mature hydrangea bushes that bordered the entire porch and walkway. In between each hanging drape, lush green ferns descended, and the table settings looked fit for royalty with elegant tall-stemmed wine glasses and gold-trimmed water glasses that matched the dishes.

Greg peeked his head out the door as the boys ran up to the porch first. "Well, if it isn't the loves of my life. Can you believe this? It's really happening, *finally*."

Michael and Steven hugged their father, glanced at the porch, then looked back at him.

Greg chuckled. "I put some games in the cellar for you two until we're ready to eat."

Michael yelped. "Awesome! Let us know when dinner's ready."

Liz finally walked up the steps, still in awe of the beauty before fixing her eyes on Greg, who immediately wrapped her up for a hug and a kiss.

Moments later, the carpools of family and friends arrived, including Margaret, Dave, and the girls, Judy and Bob, Sarah and Chris, Donna and Dale, Greg's parents, and other friends and some more kids. It was a packed house, and everyone got the full tour so Greg could proudly show off his masterpiece.

Dale stopped by the kitchen to say his hellos. Everyone except for Chef Ron had been mentored for a couple of weeks by him and his staff at Porridge, his restaurant in Collingswood. It was his way of helping Greg get off on the right foot. So far, Dale could tell it was paying off. The kitchen was running like a well-oiled machine.

By 8 p.m., after the water glasses had been filled and Chefs Ron and Mike and the kitchen staff had prepared the starting food to be served, Greg announced that it was time to take a seat.

After everyone found a chair, Greg stood between the tables and clinked a wine glass with a spoon to get their attention. "I want to thank each and every one of you for coming to my soft opening. As you know, this is something restaurant owners do to maybe get some improvement advice before the big opening, on top of just enjoying the restaurant for the first time with those who matter most. I look forward to hearing how you like everything. The servers will be by to get your orders shortly."

Everyone clapped, then looked starry eyed towards the elegantly plated first course of salad and appetizers and baskets of freshly baked breads with basil butter that Greg had the staff deliver to each table before anyone ordered.

Just as everyone was about to dig in to their salads, lit by romantic tea lights, Greg flicked the outdoor porch lights on, which had the brightness of high beams.

A few people shielded their eyes initially before shrugging and going back to their salad.

About twenty minutes later, the main entrées came out by way of the new waitstaff Greg had hired.

"Chicken Saltimbocca?" the server asked as he held the tray unsteadily at the front of the table.

"Oh, that's me," Donna said excitedly.

The server shakily took the dish off the tray, which looked like it was going to tip at any moment.

"Here, let me help you," Donna said as she quickly grabbed the dish from the server.

Another server came to the table with another tray. "I have a chicken marsala here."

Everyone at the table looked at each other, no one claiming the dish.

"I don't think any of us ordered that. Maybe it goes to that table over there," Liz said, growing concerned about this whole operation.

After dessert and many laughs and conversation, Greg came back out from the bustling kitchen to give his thank-yous while everyone clapped. He motioned to Liz to follow him out back.

"I think it went off without a hitch. What do you think?" Greg asked excitedly.

Liz made a caring smile. "It was great. The food was spectacular. I just have a couple areas of improvement for you."

Greg's happy expression drifted to worry. "What's that? I thought everything went well."

Liz sighed. "Well, you can't turn on those super bright porch lights while people are eating on the porch. It was way too harsh and took away from the ambiance of the tea lights. The other thing is, your servers are awfully green. A couple of them could barely carry food on a tray and they forgot what we ordered. The food was spectacular though."

Greg rolled his eyes. "I thought the servers seemed fine and I know the minute that I turn those porch lights off, people will complain that they needed their flashlights to see."

Just then, Dale met them out back with Donna. "Hey, you two. We're getting ready to leave and wanted to say goodbye."

Greg gave a big back-pat hug to Dale and Donna. "Thank you for coming. What did you think?"

Dale smiled. "Everything was great except for the porch lighting and the servers. Kill the lights, and give the servers another crash course on serving. They are very green. Have they served before?"

Liz nodded in agreement with Dale. "I just told him the same exact thing."

Greg slapped his hand onto his face and groaned. "They

are friends of friends' kids that needed work. I figured they'd be OK for the job."

Dale chuckled. "With fine dining, you want servers with experience. It can be a demanding job. Not that I don't think that your servers will learn and get better, but they have a lot of learning to do, and the guest experience is very important for whether someone will come back to your restaurant or not."

Greg took a deep breath. "Well, I guess this is why you have a soft opening, to learn this type of stuff."

CHAPTER THREE

Margaret took a deep breath as she walked around Dave's now fully furnished house. "This little beach home now has life again, Dave. I'm amazed at what you can accomplish."

Dave smiled. "You mean *we*. You redid the entire yard, helped me renovate *and* move in."

Margaret sighed. "Yeah, I guess you're right. It didn't feel like much at the time."

Dave took her hand in his. "Let's make dinner. The sun's about to set, and I'm starving."

Margaret looked at her watch. "Well, Paul does have the girls overnight. I guess I don't have anywhere to be. What were you thinking? Do you have any food in the fridge yet?"

Dave smirked then opened the fridge door wide open. "I don't know. What do you think?"

Margaret peered in and her eyes widened. "It looks like you ransacked the most beautiful items from the grocery store."

Dave winked. "I may have. Why don't you go relax on the porch and watch the sunset while I cook us something?"

Margaret hugged Dave from behind. "Oh my gosh, I love you."

Dave opened a bottle of fancy blood orange seltzer water

as Margaret hugged him, and poured them both a glass. "And here you go, my love."

Margaret happily took her drink to the front porch, making sure to keep the door open to the house, and got cozy in one of the comfy chairs complete with an ottoman that she picked out.

Dave got pots and pans out and diced vegetables while talking loud enough towards the front porch for Margaret to hear. "You know, I think I'm really going to love living here. The commute's longer to work, but I think it'll be worth it."

Margaret nodded and took a sip of her bubbly seltzer. "I agree. People dream of having a home like this, right on the beach and water."

It was quiet in the kitchen as Dave cooked, but wanting to talk, he chimed in again. "You know, I could see myself staying here forever."

Margaret nearly choked on her drink. "*Forever?*"

Dave added some butter to a hot pan causing it to sizzle, then he threw in the vegetables. "Yeah. I can just envision it in my head. Getting up with my morning coffee and walking along the beach as I drink it, letting the air and sunshine clear my mind and lungs. Enjoying the day. Making a meal in the backyard on the grill, then eating it outside on the patio. Taking in the sunset on the front porch, just like you're doing. Do you see it?"

Margaret's stomach formed knots. Nowhere in his forever synopsis had it included Margaret or the girls. Not to mention, was he not serious enough about their relationship to want to include her in his forever plans? She somewhat preferred having a yard large enough for a garden, even if she did have one on Liz and Greg's property.

After Margaret didn't answer, Dave called out to her. "Marg, you there?"

Margaret snapped out of her deep thought. "Oh, yes. I'm here. Sorry, I was thinking about something."

By now, the sun had completely set on the horizon, and the dark night sky along with the moon had taken its place.

Dave furrowed his brow, curious what she was so deep in thought about. "Well, dinner should be ready in about thirty minutes. I think you'll love it."

Margaret took the last swig of her drink and stood up on the porch. "Hey, Dave. I'm going to go take a drive to the ocean for a beach walk. I love the bayfront beach out front, but I think the ocean is calling me."

Dave stopped what he was doing. "Oh, um … OK. I was hoping we could do that after our meal together, but that's fine. I'll see you in a bit."

Without a goodbye, all Dave heard was the screen door slam behind Margaret.

It was pretty dark out, as there weren't many street lights around and the neighbors' porch lights seemed to be turned off. As Margaret headed to her car in the driveway, she turned around one more time to look back at the house after hearing a noise.

Margaret squinted to see where it had come from before realizing it came from Chris's porch. Beneath the glow of candlelight, she saw Sarah and Chris facing each other on a bench with their fingers intertwined, kissing in between giggles, and staring into each other's eyes.

Margaret kicked a pebble before turning back to her car, opening the door, and starting the engine. "Must be nice," she said aloud to nobody. "Dave discusses forever like I'm not even in the plans, yet Chris looks ready to propose any second."

Margaret drove a little ways until she got to her favorite beach spot on Coral Ave.

She walked out onto the beach, the moon starting to peek out from a large moving cloud, casting a bright reflection on the ocean in front of her. She walked a mile or so to the left. She'd never really walked that way before on this beach, and she needed to be anywhere other than where she'd been.

After some time, she found a cozy spot on a bare piece of packed sand and sat down, staring out towards the water.

"Universe, give me some answers. What am I doing with this life?" Margaret said aloud as she gazed up at the moon and stars.

She looked back out at the ocean and right as she was about to close her eyes and take in the cool breeze, something caught her eye in the water. She squinted to get a better look.

"Is that a seal? A shark? What is that swimming all the way out there?" Margaret thought to herself.

She stood up to get better look. Walking closer to the water's edge, she was surprised when she finally realized it was a person.

"Hello! Hey! Are you OK? Do you need help?" Margaret yelled out towards them as she waved her arms in the air.

The person didn't flinch and kept swimming under the moonlight, seemingly not hearing or seeing her. Margaret was able to make out that the person wore a swim cap and was all alone far out there, but they didn't seem to be in distress.

Margaret shook her head in bewilderment. "That is pretty dangerous to be night swimming alone so far out. Aren't they afraid of sharks? Drowning?" she thought to herself.

It had already been thirty minutes, when Dave said dinner would be ready, but she was too interested in this person swimming in the ocean to notice. She had to know why they were out there. To Margaret, the ocean was beautiful and magnificent but also scary with its currents, riptides, and powerful sea creatures. Swimming in the daytime when you can see things was much different than at night.

She took a deep breath and sat back on the sand, watching the swimmer in the ocean, until she walked farther down the beach to keep up with them. This person was a good swimmer and it showed, but was it a man or a woman?

As the person steadily stroked down the coastline, Margaret kept pace on the beach. When the swimmer stopped to adjust their swim cap, Margaret eagerly awaited to see what was underneath. They pulled the swim cap off, and a large amount of hair toppled out.

"Aha! It's a woman. I was so hoping it was a woman. It takes some fearlessness to do what they're doing, and the fact that's it's a woman just makes it all the more interesting," Margaret thought to herself, and she punched her fist into the air.

By now it had been fifty minutes, and she'd just realized it. "Dave. The dinner. Oh no. I've gotta get back," she said aloud.

She felt disappointed. She'd wanted to find out who the mysterious woman was, but she had to get back, and there was no telling how long she'd be out there swimming anyway.

Margaret power walked down the beach back towards her car. Realizing again how late she was, she broke into a full-out run, her feet digging into the sand caused her calves to work extra hard.

She finally drove back and rushed into the house to find Dave sitting at a candlelit dinner table by himself looking both sad and disappointed.

Officially thirty minutes late, Dave sat looking at their cold dishes of food. "Where were you? Remember I said thirty minutes? I worked extra hard on this meal, and now it's cold. I thought you were coming back any moment. But any moment turned into thirty minutes."

Margaret sank into her seat at the table. "Dave, I'm so sorry. I lost track of time somehow. The food looks fabulous. I'm fine with eating it cold, but I can warm it up for us. You just sit there," she said as she quickly picked up their plates and popped them in the microwave.

After a few minutes, she set the steaming hot plates back down on the table, and poured a glass of wine for Dave and herself, then dimmed the lights over the table. "There, let's start over and enjoy this meal together," she said as she took a gulp of wine, but not before letting her mind wander back to the woman in the ocean and then to Dave's future plans that only seemed to involve him.

* * *

Across town, Donna scoured the local thrift store's clothing racks during their extended summer evening hours. During college, when she had very little money, she'd started thrifting her clothes, finding expensive coveted brands for a fraction of the cost. Now that she was on a strict budget due to moving back home during a divorce and starting over, she decided to give it a try again.

She happily flipped through a rack of shirts, coming to abrupt stop when a $400 new-with-tags high-end blouse caught her eye.

"You're kidding!" Donna blurted out.

She held up and examined the blouse from top to bottom, checking for any flaws to see if it was too good to be true. It was immaculate.

Another woman a rack over looked over at what Donna was holding after hearing her. "Is that a Josie Winifred top? It sure looks it."

Donna felt giddy to share her find. "Yes. I can't believe it. It's new with tags."

The woman smiled while still flipping through her rack. "That's a good find. I just sold one of those online for $100, and that was for a preowned one. You may get $150 to $200 for that. If you think you'll only wear it once or twice, you may prefer the cash instead."

Donna's eyes widened. "Really? I've been thrifting for a long time and never thought once to resell what I find."

The woman nodded. "You'd be surprised by how many people do it. It's a fun way to make a part-time or even full-time income. I do it here and there for extra cash, but I mainly like to shop for myself."

Donna furrowed her brow. "I don't know. I feel bad. Aren't I taking away from people who need these clothes more than me?"

The woman stopped and stared. "Do you see the thousands, and I mean *thousands* of clothes and other items here? You will maybe find twenty-five to fifty items worth reselling, which is a fraction of what's here. They told me they put two thousand items on the floor daily, and what they can't sell may even get put into a landfill. Trust me, you're doing a service by finding homes for these items. There is so much clothing waste in landfills out there. It's unbelievable, and there're plenty of clothes for everyone here."

Donna put the top in her cart and nodded to the woman. "Well, this has been a very enlightening conversation. What's your name, by the way? I'm Donna."

The woman held up a sweater and looked back over at Donna. "Hi, Donna. I'm Nancy. I'm sure we'll run into each other again at the thrift store. Happy hunting!"

Donna smiled and started going through the racks again. This time, she set about with more of a purpose and excitement for finding things that she could resell online as well as for herself.

The store's intercom clicked on, alerting Donna to the time. "Attention shoppers. We will be closing in ten minutes. Please bring all of your items to the cash register. Thank you."

Donna looked at her watch, not realizing two hours had passed already. She looked at her little cart full to the brim of items—mostly to resell.

"I'm going to need to find a sunny white wall to photograph these items for when I post them online. Wait a minute. I wonder if my photography light kit is still in the basement from high school," she thought to herself.

After paying for her items, she rushed home with her heavy bags and darted down to the basement, feeling energetic and excited about getting her items online as soon as possible.

There, in the corner of the basement, covered in dust and propped against the wall, was her light kit in the bag it came in. Donna grabbed it and brought it upstairs to her bedroom.

"Yes! I can't believe it. I hope it still works. My gosh, I only used this twice for photography class," she thought to herself as she set up the lights.

After plugging the cord in and hitting the on switch, the lights miraculously popped on, blinding her since she had them positioned facing herself. She turned the lights to face the white wall, took down a frame hanging on a nail, and placed one of her items on a hanger on the now free nail.

Donna quickly took a photo with her cell phone and looked at it. "It's perfect."

Three hours later, she had not only photographed all of her items, but also listed them online for sale. She promptly fell into bed fully clothed to rest her eyes. When a call woke her a few minutes later, she sat up and groggily answered.

"Hey, you. I haven't heard from you all day, so I figured I'd give you a call before I went to bed," Dale said.

Donna laid back down on the bed. "Oh, I'm sorry. I went thrifting and ended up picking up a business idea from another woman there. I spent all night photographing and listing items to resell online. Knowing my luck, nothing will sell. What's going on with you?"

"Well, it looks like the funnel cake stand on the boardwalk is a go, as well as this volleyball league Greg and I got invited into. We're starting next week after the Fourth. You'll come watch some of my games, right?" Dale asked with a chuckle.

Donna yawned. "Definitely. That sounds like fun. I can't wait to see and eat at this funnel cake stand too. How exciting."

Dale sighed. "Yeah, I feel like I haven't seen you in a while. I wish we didn't live so far from one another. I would see you every day if I could."

Donna blushed. "Well, as they say, distance makes the heart grow fonder ... or something like that."

Just then, Donna's phone made a cash register *cha-ching* noise a few times in a row.

"What in the world? I don't know what's going on with my phone," Donna said as she looked at it.

Dale chuckled. "It sounds to me like you just made a sale."

Donna sat straight up and put Dale on speaker as she clicked on the sale notifications. "What? Is this for real? I just sold three items."

"That's great. Look at you, already successful with your new business venture," Dale said proudly.

Donna laughed, feeling overwhelmed but happy. "Well, I guess now is a good time to learn how to ship things."

CHAPTER FOUR

On July 1, Bob was itching to use the tent they'd just bought.

Judy walked into the backyard in the morning hours to see what he was doing. "Why are you setting up the tent and all of the camping equipment out here?" Judy asked with surprise.

Bob stepped back from the fully assembled large family tent. "I'm just too excited to use this. I wanted to set everything up once so I'm ready when we finally go camping, which I hope is soon."

Judy unzipped the tent and walked inside. "Well, it is quite roomy in here. You even blew up the air mattress?"

Bob laughed. "Yeah, I guess you could say I went all out. I like to be prepared."

Judy stepped back out of the tent and onto their lush green grass. "Well, as a matter of fact, the reason I came out here is to tell you that Nadine and Jerry invited us to their campsite down the road for some swimming and relaxing at the campground pool and for a cookout. They said we could stay over in our tent if we wanted."

Bob's eyes widened like a twelve-year-old boy in a toy shop. "Really? I had no idea that they belonged to a campground.

We have family coming tomorrow, though. Shouldn't we be cleaning and grocery shopping?"

Judy thought for a moment. "You know, I think we need this relaxing time away before the storm. Not to say I don't love and cherish my family, but I'm sure it will keep us busy and a little tired afterwards. Not to mention, I spent all day yesterday cleaning and grocery shopping. I think we're set. Plus, we'll leave early in the morning before any family gets here."

Bob started taking down the tent. "Perfect. So, we'll just set up our tent on their site?"

Judy nodded. "Yeah, they have a nice trailer plot. They said to come any time today."

Bob hurried around. "Well, I'll be ready in an hour. I'll pack and load the car up. We should be able to get there before noon."

Judy smiled while walking back towards the house, feeling happy for Bob but also herself. This camping idea had grown on her.

An hour or so later, after everything was packed, they were in the car, heading to Salt Water Campground a mere twenty minutes away. There were campgrounds in all directions near them, as people loved an inexpensive place to stay down at the shore while having the coveted camping feel to it at the same time.

They pulled into the campground, and after some driving, finally found Nadine and Jerry's trailer.

Nadine stepped out of the large screened porch that connected to the trailer. "Welcome, you two. Can I help you unload?"

Judy stepped out of the car and gave Nadine a hug, taking in the serene location full of tall pine trees and chirping birds.

Bob popped the trunk and lugged out the tent and camping stove. "Hi, Nadine. I think we've got it. We packed light. Where's Jerry?"

Nadine chuckled, seeing that what they packed was not light at all. "Oh, he's at the pool with our friends. We can go meet him when you're done unpacking, if you'd like. I hope you brought bathing suits."

Judy smiled as she helped Bob unload the car. "Oh, we're wearing them under our clothes. This weather is unbearably hot. I can't wait to go for a swim."

After an hour of setting up the tent and putting their belongings inside of it, they all walked towards the pool together, approaching Jerry and their friends.

"Hey, Jer! Judy and Bob are here," Nadine said as she dropped her towel and beach bag on a nearby lounge chair by the pool.

Jerry, a larger Italian man with a raspy voice and a cigar hanging out of his mouth cackled. "Hey, you two. Get in this pool. It's amazing. I don't know how I'd survive this hot weather without this pool here. Oh, by the way, these are our friends: Ralph, Theresa, Roberta, Paula, Michelle, Johnny, and Eileen."

Bob and Judy waved hello and walked into the pool from the steps to go hang out with the group, along with Nadine.

"Is this your section of the pool or something?" Bob joked.

Jerry chuckled. "Actually, yeah. See those millions of kids on that end? We steer clear of them. It's not enjoyable being splashed in the face every thirty seconds, so we stick to these parts."

After some conversation with the group, what seemed like a class trip of kids arrived at the pool. About twenty of them rushed to the sides of the pool to cannonball themselves in, which happened to be all around the group.

Everyone got splashed in the face, and Jerry's cigar drooped soaking wet from his mouth.

"Do you kids have any respect?!" Jerry yelled out with anger as he shook his fist in the air.

The kids looked back at Jerry, confused by what the issue was, then quickly swam in the other direction.

The group of friends shook their heads, wiping the splashed water out of their eyes while complaining to each other.

"How many times have we petitioned to have an adults-only hour in this pool? Ten? Other campgrounds do it. Heck, my sister who lives in Nevada, her pool does it there. It's not that uncommon," Theresa said.

Judy and Bob looked at each other, silently rolling their eyes at each other. They understood the frustration. An adult hour sounded great. However, they were used to the splashes, they had grandkids after all. Maybe that's why it just wasn't that big of deal to them.

Jerry took the drooping cigar out of his mouth and placed it on the concrete outside of the pool. "Well, I'm getting my laps in. Nobody is allowed in the lap lane except the lone swimmer. I need to work off all the prosciutto I ate."

The group of friends talked while Bob and Judy half paid attention while secretly watching to see how the lap swimming would actually go.

Jerry placed his goggles on his head, got into the empty swimming lane and started his laps.

Meanwhile, Judy and Bob cringed as they watched a new group of kids, who were probably not privy to the pool rules, walk underneath the lane divider as Bob unknowingly swam towards them.

The lifeguard whaled on his whistle, alerting the kids to get out of the lap lane, but it was too late. Jerry barreled into them as he did the breaststroke. As the lifeguard told the new kids the rules, Jerry ripped his goggles off to see what had just happened.

Next thing anyone knew, he'd turned a shade of red from anger, and it looked like steam could fly out of his ears.

Jerry shook his fist in the air as he bobbed along in the water. "You kids can't be hanging out in the lap lane!"

The kids looked at Jerry and laughed, before heading away from him.

Jerry swam back to the group. "I think I'm done with the pool today. Not to mention I'm going to speak to the owners about the adult hour or rotating hours in this pool. I've had enough. Anyone hungry? Come back to our camper. I've got steaks and the fixings."

After an enjoyable dinner and hanging out with Nadine, Jerry, and the friends, it had gotten pretty late, and it was finally time for some shut eye.

Bob and Judy were pooped. There was something about sunshine and being in the water that made them sleep like babies.

They got situated on the inflatable mattress, set up nicely with sheets, comforter and multiple pillows, before quickly falling asleep to the sound of owls hooting and nearby camp-fires crackling.

Around 2 a.m., Bob woke up abruptly, kicked the blanket a few times before screaming loud enough for the entire camp-ground to hear.

"Judy, get out of the tent! There's a snake in here!" Bob said as he ran full speed toward the zippered opening.

Judy awoke, scared out of her mind. "What's going on, Bob?"

Bob unzipped the tent and dashed outside. "Just get out now! There's a snake in our bed!"

Judy screamed even louder than Bob had and raced out behind Bob. "And you left me with the snake, Bob?"

Bob peered inside the tent while Judy looked around the completely quiet campground, everyone still snoozing. It looked like their screaming hadn't disturbed anyone.

"Well, what are we going to do, Bob? Just sleep out here with the bugs? We need to get it out."

A shiver went down Bob's spine. "Oh, you know I hate snakes. Have ever since I was a little boy. Where's Harper when we need her? Doesn't she love snakes?"

Judy bit her lip. "Just go in there with a stick or something. Maybe coax it out that way."

Bob searched around for a large stick, feeling befuddled. "How on earth did a snake get in this tent? It has been zippered shut the entire time before we got in it. Is there a hole I'm not aware of?

Judy lightly pushed him. "Bob, I don't know, but I need my sleep. Go in there and get it."

Bob tiptoed into the tent, holding his stick like his life depended on it despite the fact that he shook from top to bottom. He couldn't remember the last time he'd been so scared. He stabbed the air mattress with the stick. Then again. No movement. Then, he picked up the comforter and tossed it to the other side of the tent, holding his stick at the ready to move the snake.

Judy peered in, hesitantly. "Did you get it?"

There was silence, and then laughter. "Yeah, I found it alright," Bob said sarcastically.

Judy peered again into the tent. "Well, can you get it out? Why are you laughing?"

Bob, still laughing, walked in the dark towards Judy with something long and dangling in his hands.

"My belt. It was my belt all along. When I unpacked, I left it on the air mattress, and put the comforter on top of it," Bob said feeling embarrassed yet relieved.

Judy shook her head in annoyance, but began laughing so hard that tears welled in her eyes. "Wow, Bob. This is the best story for our first time camping together."

Bob looked at the belt in his hand and began laughing even louder along with Judy.

* * *

It was sunset and Margaret, Liz, Sarah, and Donna had all agreed to meet up for beach time. Liz and Margaret set it up, as they were still honoring their commitment to getting on the beach every day this summer. This time, they'd opted for one of their favorite beaches over at Cape May Point.

The ladies sat in their beach chairs while Donna opened the cooler and tossed a drink to everyone before Liz pointed out towards the ocean.

"Look! Is that a pod of dolphins right there?" she asked with excitement.

The ladies all stopped what they were doing to look, not seeing anything as the dolphins had gone back under.

Liz stood up out of her chair and walked to the shoreline. "I swear I saw them there."

Just then, the dolphins appeared again. This time, the rest of the gals walked up beside Liz to watch.

Margaret smiled as she took a sip of her drink. "I'll never get tired of seeing dolphins."

Liz stared out at the ocean. "I concur. Though, I don't think I've ever seen them at sunset. This is sort of magical."

Sarah sighed. "Chris said the dolphin and whale watching cruise boat next door to his boat has some of the best dolphin watching around. We should all go sometime."

Donna took a sip of her drink as she stared out at the ocean and the dolphins. "That's a fantastic idea. Maybe we can go on a quadruple date, all of us?"

Sarah took a long sigh again and was the only one out of the group not committing to the idea.

Margaret furrowed her brow. "How're things for you two, Sarah? You just moved in together. Has it been pretty wonderful?"

Sarah laughed and kicked a clam shell laying by her foot. Then, she laughed some more before tears welled up in her eyes.

Unsure of what to do, the ladies made feeble attempts to laugh along with her.

Eventually, the laughing tears streamed down Sarah's face.

Sarah finally stopped laughing and used the back of her arm to wipe her face. "To be honest, guys, I don't know whether to laugh or cry at that question. I think I just did a little of both."

"Do you want to talk about it?" Liz asked.

Sarah nodded her head. "Yeah, but do you mind if we walk the beach while I talk? I feel like it will help me clear my mind."

The group walked towards the sunset, leaving four sets of footprints behind them near the water's edge.

Sarah took a deep breath. "I'm absolutely, positively in love with Chris. Every moment has been wonderful with him, but I'm starting to realize some issues since moving in with him that are a huge turn off."

Surprised, Margaret widened her eyes. "Really? I'm shocked. Every time I see you two, it seems like a match made in heaven."

Sarah half chuckled. "I really think we are, but guys ... he's a slob. Now I'm not talking about a small mess here or there. I'm talking full-out slob."

Liz giggled. "A lot of men can be that way. Then again, Greg is the clean one and I'm more of the slob."

Sarah stopped in her tracks. "You don't understand. I've never lived with a man until him. I'm used to having everything neat and organized. I've never seen someone treat their home this way!"

The group laughed, assuming Sarah was being dramatic.

"Well, how bad is it?" Margaret asked curiously.

Sarah started walking again and the group followed. "Well, the toilet seat is constantly left up ...."

The group moaned in unison.

"We've all dealt with that. What else you got?" Donna asked.

Sarah stopped walking again and took a deep sigh. "OK, well you asked for it. I hope you have time because I'm going to be here a while. He leaves his dirty tissues everywhere. He never throws them out. They were all over the coffee table, the bed, beside the trash cans—I found one inside the fridge! How did it even get in there?

"That's not the only thing he leaves everywhere. Let's talk about his million pairs of shoes. They are strewn throughout the house, and not in a neat, orderly fashion. They are thrown about in the middle of the living room floor, the bedroom floor, and the dining room floor. It's like he comes in and flings them off to wherever they may land, like a little kid would do. I got up in the middle of the night to pee, and not being able to see where I was walking, I tripped over a set of boots that were placed—wait for this—in the middle of the bedroom floor."

Margaret couldn't help but laugh at the absurdity of the situation.

Sarah continued on. "Oh, you think that's funny? I've got more. He has a nice big standing hamper, but he never uses it. His dirty clothes are piled *next* to it or on the chair in the bedroom and in piles next to the washing machine. All he has to do is put it in the hamper! Why is that hard? I feel like I'm living in a barn.

"Oh yeah, another thing is he never cleans out his fridge, like *ever*. I found food that expired months ago in there. His crisper drawer had tons of rotten and moldy produce in it. It's just gross. I can't take it, guys."

Donna shook her head. "I have to admit. Adam, my ex, was kind of like this, but not to this extreme. You never noticed he was like this before you moved in?"

Sarah rolled her eyes. "Nope. You know why? I think he tidied up because I was coming over and he wanted to impress me. Now that we're official and living together, he has gotten a little too comfortable with our situation. Did he live like this with his ex-wife? I honestly can't see anyone being OK with this unless she was just as much of a slob as him."

Margaret shrugged. "You need to talk to him. Communication is key in relationships."

Liz and Donna nodded in agreement.

Sarah groaned. "I know, I know. I'm not looking forward to it. While I can't live like this, I'm also afraid of what might happen when I say something. Everything else besides this has been magical and wonderful. It really has."

CHAPTER FIVE

"Well, get on over here and give me a hug," Aunt Linda bellowed as she lugged her suitcases alongside her husband, Mike, into Margaret's house.

Abby and Harper put down their books and groggily walked over to the door to greet them.

"Mom! It's 7 a.m. Are you seriously yelling into the house at people?" Audrey, Margaret and Liz's cousin, didn't hide her annoyance.

Linda gave her a glare. "What? I can't greet my family?"

Audrey just shook her head, as her husband, Rob, and their eight-year-old daughter, Bonnie, trotted in behind her.

Margaret walked down the stairs holding her hot mug of morning coffee after hearing the commotion downstairs. "Look who it is! I'm so happy to see you all."

Everyone gave Margaret, Abby, and Harper a hug before being shown to their rooms for the week.

"Aunt Linda and Uncle Mike, you'll be staying in my room. It's all clean and freshened up for you two," Margaret said, admiring her spiffy cleaning and organizing job.

"Hon, where will you be staying? We don't want to push you out of your own room," Uncle Mike, asked concerned.

Margaret waved her hand flippantly. "Oh, the girls and I will be staying at Dave's new beach house to give you all more room. I can't wait for you to see it."

A sad expression formed on Linda's face. "Oh, well I was kind of hoping we'd all be under one roof. It was just perfect being at the Seahorse last year. Now we're spread all over town."

Margaret nodded and placed her hand on Linda's shoulder. "We're still going to spend entire days together. You'll really only be here to sleep and shower. Next time, we'll figure out something where we're all under one roof again, I promise. This was just so last minute, it was the best we could do."

A smile formed on Linda's face. "I know, I know."

"Aunt Debbie and Uncle Phil are staying at Liz and Greg's with Darren and Jody and their kids, and Aunt Carol and Uncle Jack are staying at Mom and Dad's. It's our usual twenty-five-person gang. It'll be great. You all have a rental car, I saw?" Margaret asked.

Mike hung up some shirts in the closet. "Yep. A nice, roomy SUV too. It's making me want one."

Margaret smiled. "Perfect. Well, get settled in, and then we're all meeting at Liz and Greg's for a big family brunch. Wear something you don't mind getting a little dirty. I'm going to head over now with the girls to help Liz and Greg cook and get ready. I've left towels out for you, and the coffee maker is ready to go if you should want some. Just have to press start."

Mike sat on the bed and closed his eyes. "Perfect. I'm ready for a long nap after all that traveling and rushing around this morning."

* * *

By 11 a.m., family members began arriving to Liz and Greg's house. Outside, Margaret, Liz, and Judy put the finishing touches on the brunch setup.

Margaret placed some colorful zinnias from the garden in a vintage milk-glass vase at the end of the long wooden farm table, then stepped back. "I need to take a photo of this. It's beyond beautiful."

Judy put some cut sunflowers from the garden in a vase in the middle of the table while Liz went around the table pouring champagne into the champagne flutes half full of fresh-squeezed orange juice.

Greg stepped outside holding two round acacia wood serving boards full of his new brunch creations. On each rustic platter sat a homemade chocolate glazed donut with sprinkles, a mini turkey Reuben, a piece of spring frittata, and a chicken fried pork chorizo gravy biscuit.

Liz's mouth dropped open. "Hon, that looks incredible. How many did you make?"

Greg laughed as he placed them on the table. "I made enough for the adults. The kids will get something more up their alley."

Just then, Dave walked out with more of Greg's exquisite brunch creations, placing the serving trays, which resembled one-inch-thick slices of tree trunks, carefully on the table. "It's a madhouse in there. I can't hear anything or what anyone is saying due to all the yelling."

Margaret, Liz, and Judy laughed. "That's our family for you. They consider yelling to be talking."

Bob stepped outside, the cacophony surrounding him before he shut the sliding glass door behind him, turning everything outside quiet again. "Phew. Can I tell everyone to come out here now? I don't think I can take being in there much longer."

Judy looked at the lush green ivy growing over the pergola that shaded the long farmhouse table before placing the last sparkly red, white, and blue patriotic stars in with the flower vases. "Yes, dear. I think we're ready."

Bob yelled over the din for everyone to come outside. Since

the family wasn't allowed to look beforehand, as everyone made their way outside, their mouths dropped open and eyes widened in the process.

"You're kidding!" Aunt Debbie said as she walked around the table, eyeing the flowers and food.

The kids knew exactly which seats were theirs by the plates and ran towards them in excitement. Greg had made mini pancakes on skewers with strawberries, blueberries, and whipped cream in between with a side of scrambled eggs.

As the family sat down to eat, Greg stood at the head of the table and held his board of food to point out what each thing was to everyone. After he finished, everyone at the table clapped and insisted he take a bow, which Greg happily obliged in a jokester way.

Between bites and sips of mimosa, Linda looked towards Margaret. "So, you told me to wear something I don't mind getting dirty. Why is that?"

Margaret and Liz looked at each other, then smiled. "Well, we thought it'd be fun if we showed everyone the garden and how to help harvest it."

Abby and Harper chimed in. "Yes! We need to show you all our secret garden, babbling brook, and tree house. Dave made it for us."

Dave smiled. "Oh, it's just a little something I did for the kids."

After everyone finished up brunch, and a group effort was put in to clear the table and wash all of the dishes, everyone headed back outside for the farm tour and activities.

Dave and Margaret walked behind everyone with their arms around each other, smiling ear to ear. "OK, you guys. We have a little surprise," Margaret said.

The family turned around, curious what she was talking about, even Liz and Greg weren't in on it.

Dave turned his hat backwards and took the lead. "We

created a scavenger hunt around the farm for everyone, adults and kids. We want everyone to get involved."

Bob threw his hand up in the air and started walking back to the house with Uncle Phil and Uncle Jack. "Y'all have fun. We're going to go watch the game."

"Oh, no you don't! This is a family activity and we want everyone here to enjoy it together," Margaret said to her dad and uncles, who all turned right back around.

"It'll need to be a group effort—you must work as a team. Your first clue is honey," Dave said with a smile.

The entire family huddled together to discuss where they could find the clue. A light bulb went on in Liz's head. "Well, we don't have hives, but we do sell local honey in our farm stand over th—"

Before Liz could finish the sentence, the kids ran off and the adults power walked behind them towards the farm stand.

Aunt Carol looked over the farm stand as they approached, then spotted a row of honey jars on the shelf, too high for the kids to reach. A folded piece of paper was stuck in between the jars.

"Well, I've found the clue!" Aunt Carol yelled to the rest of the family, who were half looking for the clue and half admiring the beautiful farm stand they'd never seen before.

Harper ran up beside Carol. "What does it say?"

Carol read the note. "It says our next clue has to do with blue tomatoes. Blue tomatoes? Do they exist?"

Audrey and Rob chuckled. "They do, you just rarely ever see them in grocery stores. Let's head towards the tomatoes in the garden," Audrey suggested.

Once in the tomato rows, the entire family walked through, admiring the colorful varieties of tomatoes growing, some towering well above them.

Aunt Linda spotted the next clue this time. A piece of paper wedged on a tomato vine surrounded by blue cherry tomatoes with a hint of yellow at the crowns.

"I've got it here!" Linda said as she waved the note. "It says our next clue has to do with morning glories. Anyone know where they are?"

Liz raised her hand. "I do! Follow me."

Everyone followed Liz to one of the flower gardens by the tree line. There, among the tall sunflowers, was a large curved trellis full of blue, purple, and pink morning glory flowering vines.

Liz and Greg's sons got to retrieve the note and did the honor of reading the next clue. "It says our next clue involves water," Steven and Michael yelled out.

The family members looked around at each other, befuddled.

Harper and Abby squealed and took off towards the tree house. "Follow us!"

The group trailed behind until they came to the beautiful, quiet spot in the woods with the tree house, brook, and fairy and flower gardens.

Everyone's eyes widened at the magical hidden spot, serene and lush, including the kids who were more interested in spending the rest of the day there instead of finding the next note.

To everyone's amazement, Margaret walked out of the tree house with a big smile.

"Mom! How did you get there already?" Harper yelled up at her.

Margaret waved. "OK, everyone. There isn't a note. I'm the note, and I will tell you your last clue. It is a tractor."

Everyone immediately left the tree house location, already knowing where the tractor was. It sat in a big wide-open field on the other side of the farm.

Once the tractor came into view, they could see Dave smiling in the driver's seat, a very large cart with tons of throw pillows for seating hooked up to the tractor.

Dave started up the motor. "Get in! There's plenty of room for everyone."

Once everyone was seated, including Margaret, Dave put the tractor in drive and they were off. To where? No one knew.

After a fun twenty-minute ride full of twists and turns and conversations and giggles, Dave pulled up to a newly cleared spot behind the tree line in a small shaded field.

Everyone turned to look, their eyes widening at this surprising and exciting little scavenger hunt Margaret and Dave put together. There, in front of them, were multiple Slip 'N Slides and many DIY carnival-like games similar to throwing the dart at the balloon, knocking the milk bottles down with a soft ball, and tossing the beanbag in the hole, among others.

The kids and some adults went to go play while the rest of the adults opted for some shady seating and conversation.

Dave hopped off the tractor, all the while smiling at Margaret.

Margaret turned her hat around backwards and ran up to him with excitement. "We did it! We really pulled it off. I managed to even keep it a secret from Liz and Greg. Don't ask how, but I did."

Dave gave her a high five and picked her up off the ground for a twirling hug. "That was too much fun. Let's do it again."

Margaret laughed while wiping the sweat off her brow. "I tell ya, the things we do for family."

* * *

Across town, Donna's reselling business had picked up speed, and she was back at the thrift store, a new normal occurrence.

She flipped through the clothing racks, when she suddenly felt a tap on her shoulder.

"Hey, Donna."

Donna spun around, still holding a blouse she was looking at. "Nancy? Hey. How are you?"

Nancy chuckled as she pointed to her full cart. "Oh, just shopping again. You know it's half-off day, right?"

Donna moved to show her full cart. "Oh, do I. You know, I want to thank you for giving me the inspiration to resell items online. I've been doing really well with it. That's why I'm here again."

Nancy smiled. "You're welcome. I'm really glad it's worked out for you. I have a full-time job at the school already, so like I said, I only resell things here or there. I mainly like to shop for myself."

Donna furrowed her brow. "The school? As in the high school?"

Nancy nodded. "Yep. I'm the history teacher and the girls softball coach."

Donna's eyes widened. "You're kidding! I played softball there. In fact, I got inducted into their Hall of Fame."

Nancy furrowed her brow before putting two and two together. "Wait a minute. Donna Blaston?"

Donna nodded. "Yep. That's my maiden name, though I am getting divorced."

Nancy's jaw dropped. "OK, so this might sound crazy, but my assistant coach just quit. We're starting a new fall ball season for the first time this year, and it's just me running it. Would you—"

Donna cut her off. "Do you need help?"

Nancy nodded. "I mean, you would still have to pass a background check and get approval, but I really could use someone like you. We've got some great girls on the team. It's a lot of fun, and you'll get paid."

Donna put her hand over her mouth. "Nancy, who are you? I mean, really. I came back home from California during a divorce with nothing, and now you've shown me how to make money on my own and offered me a job I'd love, to boot. This is insane."

Nancy giggled. "OK, I'm taking that as a yes? Give me your email. I'm going to send you over the application tonight. After that, I'll be in touch. We just started practices for the fall games."

* * *

That evening, Judy, Margaret, and Liz decided to take the family to the Ocean City Boardwalk for the first time. It was probably their favorite boardwalk, and since it was family friendly, it was definitely going to be crowded.

After driving around Ocean City looking for parking, they finally found a lot with available spots right next to the boardwalk. The family filed out of their five-car caravan and stretched their legs, ready to get some walking in.

Margaret, Dave, and the girls all held hands as they led the way up to the brightly lit boardwalk full of delicious pizza and fried food smells.

Margaret took a deep breath of air before looking up at the starry sky lit by the moon. For a fleeting second, she remembered the woman who'd swam in the ocean around this time of night. She wondered if the swimmer was out there now.

The rest of the family made their way onto the boardwalk, convening for a minute to discuss where to go.

Margaret held up some tickets. "Well, I have a ton of ride tickets for the kids, so let's head that way first."

After getting to the rides, Judy, Bob, Aunt Linda, and Uncle Mike opted to sit on a bench by the ocean across from the rides. There, they talked and people watched, happily enjoying themselves.

After an hour or so on the rides, everyone met at those benches.

"Anyone hungry? How about we introduce the family to

our favorite pizza place on the boardwalk?" Liz asked excitedly.

The kids jumped and screamed, "Yes!"

Judy, Bob, Mike, and Linda all got up to follow the family for pizza when Linda looked down at her hand.

"My wedding ring! It's gone! Where could it have gone?"

With everyone else having walked ahead towards the pizza, it was just the four of them.

"Did you take it off on the bench?" Judy asked.

"No, I did not. It was on my hand though, I know that!" Linda said, growing concerned.

Mike walked back to the bench and searched all over. Judy and Bob followed suit, even getting down on their hands and knees to peer between the wood slats and on the beach below.

"Well, it's not here, Linda. Do you think you left it at the house or in the car?" Mike asked.

Linda grew irritated. "I know for a fact it was on my hand when we got here. I was playing with. Did I just make that up in my mind?"

A loud speaker blared an announcement over the board-walk. "A ring has been turned in to the help desk. If it's yours, you must identify what it looks like before we will hand it over. Thank you very much."

Linda's eyes widened. "That has to be it. Mike, let's speed over there."

Judy shook her head. "I sure hope that's it, Linda. We'll be at the pizza place with everyone else. Meet us over there."

The large family took up many different tables in the pizza place, and huge pizza pies and birch beers took over the tables. The waiter handed out white paper plates and set a stack of napkins in the middle.

Margaret took a bite of thin oozing-with-cheese board-walk-style pizza before moaning. "It just doesn't get any better than this. The sauce has the right amount of savory and sweet. My favorite."

Judy and Bob sat across from her and Dave, and grabbed their slices.

Moments later, Linda and Mike briskly walked in and took their seats at the table.

Judy looked over at Linda. "Well?"

Linda looked at Mike and laughed. "You'll never believe where they found it."

Bob laughed. "Where was it?"

Mike shook his head. "In her pocket."

Judy tilted her head. "Wait. What? How did they find it in your pocket?"

Linda laughed while grabbing a slice of pizza. "That ring they found wasn't mine, but I did find mine in my pocket while I was there."

CHAPTER SIX

The next day, Margaret happily sat on her bike facing her large family in front of the Seahorse.

"OK, everyone! Put your helmets on and get ready for a bike tour of Cape May. Follow Dave and I, and try to keep up, but yell out to me if you need me to stop or slow down," Margaret said as she looked over the group as they got situated on their bikes, some of them having not ridden a bike in years.

Margaret and Dave led the group up the promenade, then up some tree-lined streets, making sure to ride slow for the group, who seemed to be happily bopping along while laughing and talking. The ride was meant to be relaxing, enjoyable, and not too strenuous, which was perfect for their group.

Everything had run smoothly until a crash and screams rang out from the rear of the group. They turned around to see the kids had mistakenly rode too close to some of the adults, causing a chain-reaction crash.

Everyone rushed over to help them up.

"Are you all OK?" Liz asked, giving a stern look to her sons, who'd had a part in it.

Aunt Debbie brushed herself off and looked at her arms. "I think I'm OK. Just a little banged up."

Uncle Phil helped Uncle Mike up from the ground.

"My clothes are dirty, but that's the extent of my injuries," Uncle Mike said while chuckling and brushing himself off.

Uncle Jack had already righted himself unassisted. "I'm fine, but it looks like this bike basket isn't," he said while pointing to the basket dangling by one strap instead of two on the front of the bike.

Dave quickly helped get the bikes recovered and even found a temporary fix for the basket.

Margaret sighed. "Well, we're off to a rough start, I see. Are you all still interested in going on the bike tour at this point?"

The group cheered. "Yes!"

Liz looked over at the kids. "You all have to steer clear of others. I don't want to see that happen again. It's too dangerous."

The kids nodded, apologized, and hopped back on their bikes.

Margaret resumed the tour, this time stopping in front of Heirloom. "Greg, did you want to talk about your restaurant?"

Greg rode to the front of the group, and stood on the side-walk in front of his building. "So, this is it. This is Heirloom, the restaurant I've worked on for months now. We plan to open shortly, and you will hear details about that soon."

Aunt Linda spoke up. "It's beautiful. Can we take a tour now?"

Greg sighed. "Well, I forgot my keys, and nobody else is there. Next time, but I can show you all photos when we get back to the house."

Uncle Phil spoke up from the back. "When's it opening?"

Greg cracked his knuckles. "Well, it's looking like the end of next week."

Margaret cleared her throat. "OK, everyone, follow me. We're headed down Sunset Boulevard to the next destination."

Everyone got back on their bikes and followed until they

got to a farm market set back off the road a bit. It was the same tour that Margaret gave weekly at the Seahorse, which she felt would work perfectly for her family.

Family members oohed and aahed over the beautiful lush grounds surrounding the farm market.

"Let's check out the market first, and then we can walk around the farm," Margaret said, taking Dave's hand and leading the group.

Once inside, Uncle Jack, feeling very thirsty, practically ran over to the pitchers of homemade teas and helped himself to multiple cups. "Hey, everyone. They've got complimentary tea over here. Help yourself."

Soon enough, a lot of the family had filled up cups before Margaret could say anything.

"Just so you know, that's not complimentary," Margaret said, feeling slightly concerned.

Dave stepped next to Margaret and put his arm around her. "But don't worry about it, it's our treat. Just keep track of what you drink so we can tell the cashier."

Margaret gazed up in admiration at Dave for helping her with the awkward situation.

Dave shrugged. "Eh, let's not worry about it. Your family only comes once or twice a year, right? Going a little crazy on the tea never hurt anybody."

Margaret laughed and playfully nudged Dave.

After giving the family the full tour of the vegetable and flower gardens along with introducing them to the farm animals, the group got back on their bikes and Margaret took them up the road to the winery.

Everyone followed Margaret as she glided up the winding road through the vineyards to the winery. Margaret noticed immediately that there weren't any cars in the parking lot.

"That's weird. They've never been closed when I've come here on my normal bike tours, but it sure looks it," Margaret said as she hopped off her bike and walked towards the door.

A sign was taped on it: We Apologize for any Inconvenience. Due to a Water Leak, We Will be Closed Today.

Margaret walked back to the group. "Well, today is not going exactly as planned. The winery has a water leak, so it looks like spending time here is out of the question, which is a bummer, as I wanted you all to enjoy it."

Dave thought for a moment. "You know what, I'm going to call the restaurant that the tour ends with—the one with the bread pudding—before we ride over to make sure they're open. I just have a feeling."

Margaret nodded while she tried to think of where else to take the family.

Dave got off the phone. "Well, bad news. They're open, but they have an hour and half wait. It's Fourth of July week, everything is super busy."

Margaret sighed. "Well, I have some better ideas. Are you all hungry?"

Everyone wiped the sweat off their foreheads and nodded.

"I sure am," Aunt Linda said while looking off into the distance.

Margaret hopped back on her bike. "Well, follow me. I know a place not too far from here."

Ten minutes later, they arrived at a little beach taco stand with adorable outdoor seating, and luckily plenty of it. The family put in their orders and sat in the shade, happily eating their yummy taco lunches.

Dave looked over at Margaret while enjoying his fish tacos. "So, what were you thinking for after this?"

Margaret smiled and finished her fried avocado taco. "Well, I've really had to improv here, but I was thinking the nature preserve."

Dave smiled and nodded. "Good choice."

Once everyone was done eating, they got back on their bikes and made their way to the preserve. There, they locked up their bikes, and started on the beautiful trail system bordered by thousands of wildflowers and filled with plenty of songbirds, butterflies, and bees.

Aunt Carol smiled, even though the temperature made her hot and sweaty. "It truly is gorgeous out here."

Aunt Linda walked up next to her. "You're right, but where's the shade? I'm getting too old for this hot sun."

After exploring for thirty minutes, Margaret had another idea up her sleeve, but she made sure to call first. This time, the family biked behind her to a nearby honey farm where the group was given a tour and education on the process of honey production. At the end, they were able to taste and buy some freshly made local honey.

Judy held up her honey purchase. "I bought their strawberry honey. I've never tasted anything like it. I could just eat it by the spoonful."

Bob walked next to Judy. "Well, just save some for me, honey. You know strawberries are my favorite."

By now, Margaret was enjoying the day, but felt slightly exhausted between the heat and having to figure out where to go on the bike tour on the fly.

"Are you all feeling up to one more spot before we head back?" Margaret asked curiously.

Uncle Phil placed his honey purchase in the bike basket and did a lunge stretch. "You bet. I'm loving all of this exercise."

Margaret looked around at nodding heads and smiling faces—overall, the group looked like they were generally enjoying themselves. Then, she glanced at Dave. "I guess we'll finish it up with Sunset Beach. We're too early for the sunset, but they'll love the shipwreck and Cape May diamonds."

Dave smiled and rubbed her back. "Want me to lead this time? Give you a little break? Go ride next to your cousins and enjoy yourself."

Margaret smiled. "Sure. That sounds good."

* * *

By nightfall, it had been decided that everyone would gather at Dave's place for North Cape May's annual July 3 fireworks display. It was a yearly event full of food trucks and children's rides, and of course the main event, the fireworks, where everyone gathered to watch them on the beach.

Coincidentally, Dave's neighbors had rented out their house to what looked like a group of female college students, but who could tell in this day and age.

It was 6 p.m. when the family arrived at Dave's. After getting the full tour of the house and backyard, everyone walked to the street out front to support the many vendors, and watch the kids enjoy the rides.

"I'm going to set up our fireworks-watching spot on the beach now before there aren't any left," Margaret said to the group as she walked back to the house to grab a handful of chairs.

"Wait for me," Dave said, as he hurried behind her.

Margaret smiled at this man she loved; he had taken to her large, loud family so lovingly and helped out any chance he could.

By 8:30 p.m. (after the family had eaten way too many fried Oreos, cheesesteaks, and junk food), everyone made their way down to the beach where it was already quite crowded. Luckily they had their spot secured with chairs and blankets along the water's edge.

The sunset filled the sky with an orange glow as it faded and disappeared beyond the horizon, giving way to the dark starry night. Moments after full darkness, the first firework went off from a barge in the distance. Then another and another. With eyes sparkling from the lights, the entire crowd on the beach almost felt like one big family, enjoying special things in life together.

Dave grabbed Margaret's hand as they huddled on the

54

blanket together surrounded by Abby and Harper and the rest of the family and turned away from the fireworks to look her in the eyes. Margaret looked back at him, while Dave reached for something with his other hand.

"Steven and Michael! You've walked too far. Come sit on the blanket with the rest of your cousins," Liz yelled out, interrupting Dave and Margaret's special moment .

"Oh! Do we have to? We see a couple friends from school right there," Michael said pointing.

Liz looked to Greg for his reaction, but he just shrugged it off. "Fine, but don't leave my sight. Come right back when the fireworks are over."

After the fireworks, the family went back to Dave's for some drinks and conversation in the backyard, but everything wasn't as serene and peaceful as one would hope after the crowds left.

"Where is that extremely loud music with pounding bass coming from? I can't even hear myself," Aunt Linda asked while looking around.

Judy scrunched her brow. "And the yelling and hooting and hollering. I guess someone's having a big party around here?"

"It's coming from that side," Aunt Carol said while pointing.

Dave peeked through the fence to see the college kids having a full-out, raging party. Beer pong was being played and what looked to be their entire college spilled out of the house and into the backyard.

Dave's eyes widened. "I have yet to meet the owners of that house, but I'd imagine they did not know about all of the people in their place. This is not good. They're going to tear that place up, and have the cops called on them if this goes on all night."

Greg peered through the fence next to Dave and shook his head while chuckling. "Oh, I remember those days very well. They were fun, but it won't be fun for the homeowner who will have to face the repercussions. Do you have the owner's number or anything?"

Dave shook his head. "Believe it or not, I haven't seen them at all since I moved in. I don't know what the deal is over there. Maybe they leave everything in the hands of their realtor for bookings?"

A couple more hours of conversation and yelling over the loud party at the neighbor's house, and everyone had left Dave's aside from Margret. Abby and Harper decided to stay at their house with their cousin Bonnie for a sleepover.

Margaret had gone inside to get away from the party noises when she suddenly remembered the woman swimming in the ocean. She hadn't told anyone about her yet, and frankly, she wasn't really ready to. She liked having a secret mystery to solve herself.

"I'm going to go take a quick drive to the beach. I'll be back," Margaret said as she started for the front door.

"You want me to go with you?" Dave asked curiously.

Margaret smiled. "No, I think I just want to regroup alone. Being with family all the time has made me yearn for a little solo time."

Dave nodded, understanding completely. "Sure thing. Bring your phone though. I don't want to have to worry about you."

Margaret gave him another warm smile before she stepped off the front porch and got into her car, driving back to Coral Ave. beach, and walking towards the area where she'd last seen the swimmer.

After a bit of walking, Margaret finally reached the spot where she'd been swimming before, except this time she wasn't there. She instantly felt a little bummed out. A part of her was excited to see this stranger, so she decided to walk even further down the beach, and there the swimmer was. She bobbed along with the waves in her swim cap, looking up at the moon, all alone like last time.

Margaret stood on the beach staring to get a better look and yelled out, "Hey! Hello!"

The woman turned to look in Margaret's direction, confusion spread across her face.

"Are you OK out there?" Margaret asked, not sure what to say now that she had the women's attention.

The woman flicked her hand and laughed as she floated over a large wave. "I'm fine! Don't worry about lil' ole me."

"I'm Margaret. What's your name?" Margaret yelled back to her.

There wasn't an answer as the woman had already gone back into the water to resume her laps through the ocean.

After watching the woman swim a little longer, Margaret left, as she was starting to creep her own self out. This woman probably didn't want anyone watching her, even if well-meaning.

Margaret eventually made her way back to the house, but not before seeing three cop cars parked outside of the neighbor's house with the huge party.

Dave was already standing on the front lawn watching the whole spectacle like a few of the other neighbors. "Well, I knew it was a matter of time before this happened."

"Did you call?" Margaret asked while watching the officers disperse the party.

Dave laughed. "Nope. I'm not going to be that guy. I let someone else do it, and they did. I just hope that house isn't damaged."

Margaret sighed. "Well, hopefully you can meet the owners soon if only to have their number for things like this. This is why it's important to get to know your neighbors."

Dave put his arm around Margaret. "Was your walk nice?"

Margaret smiled as they moved back into the house. "It was. I finally talked to someone I keep seeing out there with me. I didn't get her name, though."

Dave nodded and kissed her head. "Good. I'm glad."

CHAPTER SEVEN

"I hired a company to set up cabanas for us," Uncle Phil said proudly. He stood on the busy hot, sunny beach on the Fourth of July looking at the four cabanas lined up next to each other.

"You did what?" Judy said with her mouth wide open in disbelief.

"It wasn't that pricey at all, and I figured it's Fourth of July with the family and you only live once, right?" Phil said, studying the fixtures that stuck out like a sore thumb in between all of the umbrellas. There were other cabana rentals on the beach here and there, but not four in a row like their setup.

The rest of the family having lugged their beach carts, chairs, and coolers onto the beach, stopped in front of the cabanas next to Judy and Phil, wiping the sweat off their brows, and looking for a spot to set up camp.

Judy grinned. "These cabanas are ours. Uncle Phil rented them. So, X marks the spot here. Let's settle in."

The kids shrieked and ran under the cabanas like they were their own personal forts before asking to dip their toes in the water by the lifeguards.

"Wow! Thank you, Uncle Phil. This is a pleasant surprise. I

guess we don't have to worry about setting up these umbrellas we brought," Liz said as she plunked her stuff down and looked around the busy beach.

"You're welcome. Enjoy. However, I do have another surprise. Did you know that you can order food and have it delivered to the beach in little sand buckets? I have lunch coming around noon, as well," Phil said while adjusting his chair under the cabana right next to the cold drink cooler.

Aunt Linda adjusted her sunglasses and plopped down in her chair with a new book. "That's perfect, Phil. What a pleasant surprise. Thank you. We've got everything we need here. Even the bathrooms are close by. We can just relax and enjoy the beach all day."

Last to arrive on the beach was Bob, and he carried Judy's beach bag plus a few more chairs while nearly hopping in place so the hot sand wouldn't burn his feet.

Judy grabbed the beach bag from him. "Perfect. I've got all of our beach tags in my bag. They'll probably be by soon to check."

Audrey glanced over at Judy. "Beach tags? What are those for?"

Judy, realizing that New Jersey may be one of the only states that require them, reached inside her bag for a beach tag to show her, but couldn't locate any. "Well, many of NJ beaches call for them as sort of fee to use the beaches. It helps with the maintenance of running the beach when it comes to things like restrooms and lifeguards."

Audrey nodded, then plunked her stuff down under the cabana.

After rummaging through the bag for a few more minutes, Judy looked up at Bob with concern on her face. "The beach tags. They're not in here. I think I left them in the plastic baggie on the dining room table."

Bob shook his head and sighed in exasperation. "OK, dear. I'll go back and get them."

Judy kissed him on the cheek. "You're a saint, you know that?"

Bob chuckled. "I may be, but I don't know if the beach tag checkers are going to fall for your story of leaving this many people's tags at home. You'd better have a backup plan."

Just then, Chris, Sarah, Donna, and Dale arrived, having been invited by Margaret.

Margaret greeted them and turned back to the rest of her family who were still applying sunblock and getting situated under the cabanas. "Hey, everyone, you know Sarah. This is her boyfriend, Chris, and this my friend Donna and Dale."

The family said their hellos, waved, and went back to what they were doing.

Judy walked up to Margaret. "So, I left all the beach tags on the dining room table for the family. Do you have yours?"

Margaret nodded. "I do, but only for the four of us. Will Dad be back in time before they come check us for them?"

Judy shook her head and looked down the beach. "I don't think so because they're right there."

Margaret did some quick thinking, then made an announcement. "OK, everyone. Stop what you're doing. Let's go to the water's edge for a little walk and family photo."

There was some groaning at the suggestion of getting up after having just got comfy, but everyone obliged, and in the nick of time.

By the time the photo was taken and they'd walked back, Bob had returned with everyone's beach tag. Upon seeing the large group, the beach tag collectors turned around to check, and Bob happily held up the many beach tags to them.

Judy smiled and sat in her chair under the cabana. "Thank you, Margaret!"

While the family chitchatted, Dave, Dale, Greg, and Chris found an empty volleyball net not too far away and decided to have a little pickup game since Dale had brought a volleyball.

That left Margaret, Liz, Sarah, and Donna alone to have some gal time, which was perfect for some life updating.

Everyone looked over at Donna first, curious how life was going since moving back to Cape May and dating Greg's friend Dale.

"Are you still doing the thrifting thing, Donna?" Margaret asked.

Donna nodded and leaned back in her chair. "Oh, boy am I. I'm making more than I was at my old job in California and working less to boot. Not to mention, searching thrift stores feels like I'm looking for buried pirate's treasure. It's become Zen-like for me. I absolutely enjoy it. I've started getting into glassware, too."

"You're kidding?" Liz said, feeling excited for her friend.

Donna spread some sunblock on her arms. "It's really funny how things work out sometimes. I would have never known to do this, but I ran into another woman at the thrift named Nancy, who brought it up to me. Now, get this …."

The rest of the group leaned forward ready to hear what she had to say.

"I ran into Nancy again, and we struck up a conversation about what she did for a living. She teaches at our old high school, and she's the head softball coach. So, naturally that brought up how I used to be the star softball player in the school and how I was inducted into the Hall of Fame with my own banner in the gym that still hangs today," Donna said while glancing over at Dale, admiring how cute he looked landing in the sand while spiking the volleyball.

Sarah's mouth dropped open. "What a coincidence. Wait did she ask you to—"

Donna nodded. "Yes, she did. She asked me to help out as an assistant coach for the fall softball team, a new seasonal thing they're trying. I had to apply first to get screened and so forth, but I'm having a good feeling about it. It's paid too. Nothing crazy, but I'm just excited to get involved again."

Margaret got up out of her chair and bent over to give Donna a big hug. "You don't know how happy I am for you right now. Everything is turning out wonderfully for you so far. Are you still playing guitar too?"

Donna glanced at Dale again, this time their eyes caught and they smiled at each other. "Yes, I've been playing with Dale a lot, just the two of us. He's asked me to join in on jam sessions with his band, but I haven't had any desire yet. We'll see. There is one other thing that's happened … though not necessarily good."

Liz furrowed her brow. "Oh? What's that."

"Well, I talked to Adam for the first time since moving back. Like, really talked. He's having second thoughts about staying in California. He mentioned wanting to come back to Cape May," Donna said, while glancing back at Dale.

"Did you tell Dale?" Margaret asked curiously.

"No, not yet. There's nothing really to tell since nothing was set it stone, and honestly, I don't know how important it is. I just found it interesting that he all of a sudden wants to come back to his hometown when he never did all of those years," Donna said rolling her eyes. "OK, enough about me for now, who's next?"

Nobody said anything, as they became preoccupied with checking their phones and looking to see where their children were.

"Well, one of you better get to talking. I just spilled everything. How about you, Sarah?" Donna asked.

Sarah put her phone back in her beach bag after checking it briefly and smiled.

"Well, Chris is still the messiest person ever. There's that," Sarah said, laughing.

Margaret rolled her eyes. "You never talked with him? You need to get on that. I don't know how you live with all those dirty tissues everywhere."

Sarah let out a long sigh. "I know. I just haven't had the

heart to say anything yet, but I'm going to have to soon. I can't live like this."

Liz leaned forward in her chair and propped her chin in her hands. "How is everything else when it comes to living together? Are you happy?"

Sarah leaned back in her chair, a smile overcoming her face. "Aside from that fact that Chris can be a major slob, everything else is dreamy. Like, really. Wonderful, even."

Donna widened her eyes. "Really? Do tell."

Sarah exhaled another long sigh, but more of a happy relieved one this time. "Well, we have this sort of schedule, and it's just the most amazing thing. On Mondays, we work the sunset boat tour together. On Tuesdays, we get Chinese take-out, then snuggle up together on the couch with hot Sleepy-time tea, watching old movies until we fall asleep. On Wednesdays, we usually grill dinner and play board games with his son, Sam, afterwards. On Thursdays, Chris helps me make deliveries for the Monarch Coffeehouse to local customers and afterwards we make tacos and go for a long walk on the beach, then watch the sunset from the porch. On Fridays, we usually go out to eat somewhere, then pay visits to our parents. I could go on and on. Some may think this routine sounds monotonous and boring, but I have to say it brings me so much joy. Obviously, we can change it up whenever we want or be spontaneous, but right now, it just feels so right."

The rest of the ladies nodded and smiled, feeling both slightly jealous and inspired by the comfy, cozy schedule Sarah had.

"What about you, Liz? How's everything?" Sarah asked.

Liz sighed, feeling overwhelmed at the windstorm of stuff going on as soon as the Fourth of July holiday with the family was over. "Well, I've been offered a nice payment to do the interior design of that new local hotel, The Sand Pit. I start this weekend, as soon as our family leaves. I was feeling over-whelmed at first at the thought of taking on this job, but it's only for a month, and right now the Seahorse is being mainly run by our employees, who are doing a fabulous job. So, really, I *can* take this on. I'm just nervous."

Donna furrowed her brow. "Why are you nervous?"

Liz sighed. "I don't know. I've never really taken on a commercial design job. I've only worked with residential clients. This is much bigger than anything I've ever worked on."

Margaret smiled. "I'm sure you'll be fine. You're fantastic at what you do. How's Greg and the restaurant coming along?"

Liz looked over at Greg happily playing volleyball with the guys. "Well, I think he's worked out the kinks with his green staff. He's put them through some better training, and took a lot of pointers from Dale, which was wonderful. He's hoping to open by the end of this week. I'm so excited for him, especially after all the ups and downs he's had getting it up and running."

Sarah dug her toes into the sand and took a sip of her drink. "That's really great. Will his side of the family be coming to the opening since they weren't at the soft opening?"

Liz rolled her eyes. "About that ... yeah. Well, his parents, yes. They were at the soft opening and will be coming to the opening as well. However, I'm not sure about his brothers or sister. There's always been distance between me and his siblings. It's not that we don't get along, but we've never bonded. His sister lives out of state, and well, his brothers, let just say we're very ... different. I've invited them to different family functions, and they've always declined. It's very strange."

Donna furrowed her brow. "That's weird. Is Greg close with them?"

Liz shook her head. "Not really. They never call or ask about our sons. They seem so engrossed in their own lives that they just don't care about anyone else. It bothers Greg, but I think having my family has helped to fill that void. Greg loves my entire family. It's his family now since we got married."

Margaret nodded. "And we love Greg. He's the brother I never had."

Liz smiled. "He appreciates that, Margaret."

Sarah crinkled her nose. "So, what are his brothers' wives like? I'm surprised they don't put any effort into a relationship with you two."

Liz laughed. "They're the issue. I don't think they like me. Maybe I'm the reason that Greg isn't close to his brothers. Both of his brothers' wives unfriended me on social media years ago for no reason at all. We've never not gotten along. It was just this sudden unexpected thing. You know, I don't think I want those kinds of people in my life anyway."

Margaret threw a drink to Liz. "You're my sister and you're amazing. Don't ever let those stuck-up wives get to you. Ignore them and live your life."

Liz smiled while catching the drink. "That's the plan."

Margaret cleared her throat. "OK, I guess it's my turn."

Donna adjusted her sunglasses. "Yes, we need to hear about Margaret now and that beach house!"

Margaret smiled. "Well, the girls and I have been staying with Dave this week—the first time we've all temporarily lived together, and it's been really, really nice. I know it's only been a few days, but so far it's everything I dreamed it would be."

Sarah laughed. "Well, I hope you don't get my surprise situation."

Margaret shook her head. "I don't think I will. Dave has always talked about what a neat freak he was, and he's been pretty true to his word so far."

"Are you still working from home for Pine Tree Wildlife Refuge?" Donna asked.

Margaret nodded. "Yep. Still doing that full-time. I had thought about doing it part-time for a while, especially after we opened the Seahorse, but once we let our employees take the reins this summer, I've been glad I didn't."

Liz furrowed her brow, having heard this for the first time. "Why's that?"

Margaret glanced at the kids now playing in the sand close by. "Well, I love my job at the refuge, and I really didn't want to give it up, but I was worried that I would have to in order to run our B&B. Turns out, hiring employees to help run the Seahorse has been one of the best decisions ever. I mean, we're still making a profit, still have our regular jobs, and still have time to be with our family and friends and sit on the beach. I feel like it's a win-win."

Liz smiled. "I'm glad we made that decision too."

Sarah leaned forward on her chair. "I want to know more about you and Dave. Do you think he's going to propose anytime soon?"

Margaret laughed. "No, I don't. We haven't even discussed moving in together yet. Frankly, I was a little upset the other night when he started discussing the future as though I wasn't in it."

Donna shook her head. "I'm sure he sees you in it. It probably just came out wrong. We can all see plain as day that the man is head over heels for you."

Margaret sighed and looked to where the guys played volleyball. Having caught Dave's eye, he smiled and waved to her. "Well, I hope you're right, but I just don't know. He hasn't mentioned us living together once, which is odd to me."

Liz sat up. "Look, you have it good. All of Dave's siblings and their spouses like you. That's a better start than I had."

Margaret took a sip of her drink. "Yeah, I guess that's something. It's funny. Paul, my ex, gets along better with Dave than I do now. Last Christmas they bonded, and now whenever Paul drops the girls off and Dave is there, they end up standing outside talking for thirty minutes about who knows what."

Sarah looked over at the guys and chuckled. "Um, I think they're motioning for us to go play with them."

Donna raised her sunglasses off her eyes. "What? I don't know how to play."

Liz removed her short sleeve shirt from over her bathing suit. "Who cares. Let's go show 'em how it's done."

Margaret chuckled. "Oh yeah. I forgot that you got super into volleyball that one year. Well, let's not get too worn out. Remember, we have Fourth of July fireworks tonight."

Sarah quickly put some sunblock on her chest and arms. "Can't the fireworks be seen from this beach? Let's just stay here until they're over."

Liz laughed while walking towards the net. "I don't ever see that happening with this family. We love our cold showers after a hot day on the beach too much. We may even have to fit in some miniature golf before the fireworks tonight too."

CHAPTER EIGHT

Fourth of July week had gone by quickly, and funny enough, most of the visiting family was still there a day later than expected. At least the retired portion of the family who had driven in and had more flexibility was.

Judy and Bob discussed their next camping trip to Assateague Island during breakfast at the noisy local diner with their family while they were all squished into an extra-large wraparound booth.

"So, you're going on a camping trip in a couple days?" Aunt Linda asked, taking a bite of her omelet.

Bob nodded and took a sip of his hot coffee. "Well, where we are going is Assateague Island in Maryland. It has camping spots right on the beach. You can wake up in the morning and see the ocean and the wild horses walking on the beach. There're great little walking trails and nearby is Ocean City, which has lots of great restaurants and things to do for a change of scenery if needed. It sounds dreamy, doesn't it?"

Uncle Mike closed his eyes and took a sip of his coffee. "I'll say. Linda and I used to take the kids camping all the time when they were little. I miss it so. I'm not sure when we'll get to do it again."

Aunt Carol bit her lip in thought. "Well, would you two want company on your camping trip? I kind of want to go. Jack, wouldn't you like to go camping?"

Uncle Jack nodded. "Well, I've never camped on a beach. It does sound interesting."

Judy clapped her hands together. "We would *love* for you all to come. We'll have to go shopping to get you all tents and air mattresses and such, though. I have sheets and blankets and extra pillows for you. Would you be up for all of that?"

Aunt Debbie took a bite of her French toast. "Sounds good to me. We drove so we can take everything home with us without any issues. It's not like we have to worry about flying home with it."

Bob clapped his hands one time. "Then, it's set. We're all going camping together in a couple days. Let's get to shopping and planning. I'm excited."

* * *

Across town, Liz arrived for her first day of interior designing at The Sand Pit. She walked into the hotel with her laptop satchel across her body and creativity coursing through her veins. She stopped in the empty lobby and did a 360-degree turn as she took everything in. It hadn't been that long since she'd been there, but she had forgotten some structural details.

She took a small notepad and pen out of her bag to jot ideas down when a young woman walked into the room.

"Hi. You must be Liz. I'm Melody," she said as she extended her hand.

"Hi, Melody. I was hired by Fred. I'm just getting some ideas for the space," Liz said as she went back to writing on her notepad.

Melody pursed her lips. "I'm his niece. I'm the one who originally designed all of this."

Liz stopped writing. "Oh."

Melody crossed her arms. "I guess he didn't fancy my simplistic style for the hotel. I recently graduated from college with my interior design degree."

Liz nodded her head, feeling a little awkward. "Well, it sure is a minimalist style that's going on here."

Melody nodded her head. "Right. Well, it's what's in right now. Less clutter, more clean spaces."

Liz rolled her eyes on the inside. "Yes, but some things can be too minimalist, even for hotels. There needs to be a structure of some sort that guests recognize as the check-in area when they arrive to the hotel. A big empty lobby isn't really conducive to appealing to the demographic that will be staying here."

Melody put her hand on her hip. "Well, whatever. I think it's fine. However, my uncle wants me to help you. So, we'll be working together."

Liz put her notepad in her back pocket and the pen behind her ear and laughed. "Yeah, no. I told Fred that I would only work on this hotel under the condition that I do so alone. I do this full time, and I never work with anyone."

Melody started to speak, but was interrupted when Fred walked into the room.

"Fantastic. I see you've met my niece. Liz, I think you two will work wonderfully together," Fred said as he adjusted some blinds.

Liz shook her head. "Fred. We've already discussed this. I work alone. I took the job on that condition—we agreed on that."

Fred sighed. "I know, I know. However, I owe this to Melody. She's my niece, and she's already put so much work into this hotel. Maybe she could even learn a thing or two from you."

Melody rolled her eyes. "Learn from *her*. Yeah, OK. She probably graduated college eons ago when they were teaching way outdated styles. I just finished college learning about all the hip new trends that everyone wants."

Liz squinted her eyes at Melody in disbelief. "Well, while you were in college learning, I was out in the field working. I know about everything that is in because I work in the field … getting paid."

Fred clapped his hands together. "OK, well, we've got a month to get this hotel looking it's best. Why don't you two exchange numbers and we can all put our heads together."

Melody shook her head. "Uncle Fred. I don't think this is going to work out."

Fred stopped and turned to Melody. "I think it's in your best interest to work alongside Liz. You'll still be paid, and Liz, I'll bump your pay up for doing this."

Liz and Melody both sighed in unison. "OK, fine. But only for a month," they both said simultaneously while looking at each other.

Melody sighed again then left the room to go get her notebooks and laptop.

Meanwhile, Fred stayed back with Liz. "Look, I'm so sorry to spring this on you. I just didn't have the heart to pull my niece off this job. I had to include her somehow."

Liz sighed while getting busy jotting notes about the space on her notepad again. "I hope we don't kill each other in the process, Fred."

* * *

Over on the Wildwood Boardwalk, Dale put the finishing touches on his new gourmet funnel cake cart and went over a few things for his new hires, some high school and college kids looking for summer work.

"Johnny! What are you doing? You make the funnel cake like this," Tammy said while giggling and grabbing the squeeze bottle full of batter.

Johnny chuckled and stepped back to let Tammy make the funnel cake, but not before checking her out.

Dale rolled his eyes, wondering if hiring such young workers was in the best interest of his business.

"Tammy, the apple pie filling is over here if you need it," Johnny said with a wide toothy smile.

Tammy whipped around with the batter bottle, accidentally squeezing it and spraying it all over Johnny and the wall behind them.

"Oh. My. Gosh. Did I just do that?" Tammy said, sounding slightly shocked, but still not able to contain her laughter.

Johnny wrestled her for the bottle, knocking over items on the cart in the process, while Dale kneeled on the ground outside, trying to fix a cosmetic issue on the cart's signage.

"What is going on back there?" Dale asked feeling slightly annoyed at their immaturity.

"Nothing!" Johnny and Tammy both said in unison before breaking into hysterical giggle fits.

Dale took a deep breath and looked around at the other nearby carts to see who was working them. They were mostly young workers as well. The job was a seasonal summer position, and not many adults were in the market for short-term summer jobs like students were. It was what it was.

He stood up from the ground and dusted himself off before peeking inside the cart. "Are you guys ready? I mean really ready? I'm about to officially open the cart."

Tammy and Johnny both nodded, while scrambling to organize and remember everything from the training Dale had already done with them days prior.

Dale nodded and walked to the front of the cart where he opened the order window and turned the closed sign around to open.

"Well, I think business may be a little slow today. Not many people know about us yet. So, that might be a good thing.

You'll get an easy day to learn the ropes," Dale said while looking around the busy boardwalk.

Tammy looked out the order window towards the ocean. "This is the best summer job ever. I'm going to go lay out on the beach as soon as my shift is over."

Johnny crinkled his brow. "Maybe I'll do the same. Want some company?"

Tammy looked over at Johnny and smiled. "Perhaps."

Dale peeked inside the cart and adjusted a few things. "Are you two going to be OK if I split? Do you think you have a handle on this? We went over everything like three times, right?"

Tammy and Johnny nodded as an entire school swim team walked up to the cart to read the menu with squinted eyes, then they all lined up to order—all twenty of them.

Tammy took each order and rang them up, and Johnny got to work on the funnel cakes, but he kept overcooking them, so he had to start over.

Dale, getting nervous about their first impression, hopped in the cart and took over on making the funnel cakes, frying them up and flipping them while Johnny dressed each one with toppings before giving it the customer.

After fifteen minutes, they were exhausted, but the entire swim team got their fancy funnel cakes dressed with cherry compote or Oreos or homemade apple pie filling among many other delicious toppings.

Dale took off the apron he'd thrown on and wiped the sweat from his brow. "That was something. I'm glad I stayed. I really should be here for the first day of the cart being open."

Tammy and Johnny nodded, then high-fived, feeling proud of how they'd all worked together as a team.

Dale went on. "However, while we wait for our next orders, we need to go over the proper way to fry the funnel cake so you can do this without me in the future."

After hours of working the busy stand and retraining his

employees, it was dark out and finally time to close up shop. Greg met Dale on the boardwalk.

"Hey. How did it go?" Greg asked as he stood holding a volleyball.

Dale couldn't wipe the exhaustion off his face. "Well, I was only supposed to be here an hour or so, and ended up having a super busy first day so I stayed. Are we really doing this volleyball game tonight? I'm so tired."

Greg chuckled. "Yep. They even have lights over the nets. You want to cancel? You're probably wanting to get home and relax I bet."

Dale thought for a moment. "You know. I'm going to stick it out. It's our first time playing with these guys, I want to see what it's all about. Maybe I'll get a second wind," Dale said as he quickly changed into a different shirt.

Greg tossed the ball to Dale. "Alright, cool. You ready to head down to the beach?"

Dale rubbed his eyes and yawned. "I think so."

As they walked down the boardwalk and out onto the beach where the volleyball net was, they soon realized they were the oldest guys there. Most of the guys on the team looked like they were in their early twenties, with the two guys they met being in their thirties.

Dale rubbed his eyes again. "This is making me feel really old, Greg. Are we the grandpas on this team?"

Greg laughed and nudged. "Come on. Let's just play. I bet it will be fun."

They introduced themselves to the guys, who were all so welcoming and friendly, and after some discussion, they picked teams and started up the game.

After an hour or so, everyone shook hands, discussed the next game date and place, and went their separate ways.

Dale and Greg walked back to their cars together, with Dale tossing the volleyball to himself the entire way. "Today has got to be one of the most tiring—but rewarding—days I've had in a while. I feel so productive and accomplished. I'm glad we did this."

Greg laughed. "Yeah, I was thinking those young guys were going to show us up, but overall, I think we all played pretty decently. I even got some good spikes in and surprised myself. I'm excited for the next game. It's great to be able to do something outside of the restaurant for a change."

Dale patted Greg's back. "I feel you on that. I'm going to tell you something, though. I'm thinking about moving down here."

Greg looked over at Dale with confusion on his face. "You are? How's that going to work with your restaurant being over an hour away in Collingswood? Won't that be too long of a commute every day?"

Dale smiled. "Well, I'm working on figuring all of that out. You'll see."

Greg scratched his head. "So, is this because of Donna?"

Dale turned red. "Well, I mean sort of. She doesn't know anything about this yet. I haven't told her about it."

Greg smiled. "So, you really like her, eh? You think she's the one?"

Dale sighed. "I'll say this. I *really* like her, and I constantly think about her when I'm not with her. I'm so much happier when I'm down here in Cape May. I don't know if it's Donna or the mixture of love, the beach, my friends, the sunsets, the amazing restaurants, the many opportunities—"

Greg furrowed his brow. "Opportunities?"

Dale nodded. "Yeah, there have been some opportunities besides the funnel cake cart. I'm just not ready to tell Donna about this all yet. Don't tell Liz or anyone else."

"I definitely won't. You have my word," Greg said.

CHAPTER NINE

A day later, Donna finished up her shipments for everything she'd sold over the past couple of days. One hundred items to be exact. She was becoming addicted to thrifting and the thrill of the find—and making money from it was the icing on top.

She placed her ball cap over her ponytail and adjusted her short-sleeved polo shirt and khaki shorts before saying goodbye to her parents and heading out the door for her first practice as the assistant softball coach.

Upon arriving, she was greeted by Nancy who had already started the girls on throwing and catching warm-ups. "Hey, Donna. Beautiful day, isn't it? Not sweltering like usual. Makes for a fine day for practice."

Donna put her sunglasses on. It wasn't as hot, but it sure was sunny. "Yes, it's wonderful out. How are we going to do practices when it does get sweltering again? Maybe have some night practices under the lights?"

Nancy nodded. "I already asked permission to do that. Problem is, some of the boys baseball leagues practice on the fields we would use at night. I think we could squeeze in some-how, though."

Donna observed the girls catching and throwing. Most of them weren't throwing properly or even catching the ball very well. One girl nearly got smacked in the face with the ball when she stopped to look at her phone.

Nancy sighed. "They need a lot of work, as you can tell. I told them not to bring their phones on the field, but some of them don't listen."

Donna furrowed her brow. "Yeah, we need to make some changes around here. Do you mind if I take the lead today? It's been a while since I played, but I sure remember what worked for me and my team back then in terms of getting us to be better players."

Nancy shrugged. "Sure. Have at it. I'd like to see what you have up your sleeve."

Donna smiled and jogged towards the girls, scooping a loose rolling ball in the process and throwing it towards a girl staring up at the sky. "Heads up!"

The girl finally came to and managed to put her glove out and catch the ball in the nick of time. "You almost hit me with that."

Donna laughed. "What's your name? You can't be staring up at the sky during softball practice. Rule number one."

The girl blew a big pink bubble and snapped it. "I'm Jackie. And you are?"

"I'm Donna, the new assistant coach. I used to play softball at here years ago. I know a thing or two."

Jackie shrugged, not sure what to say. "Well, OK. Maybe you can help us get better. We were the worst team out all of the high schools during the spring. Like, literally the worst. We won one game."

Another girl walked next to Darlene with her glove. "She's not lying. Even the team with a missing player beat us. I'm Stacy, by the way."

Donna smiled. "Nice to meet you, Stacy. Now if you hold

on a second, I'm going to make an announcement to everyone else."

Donna cupped her hands around her mouth and yelled to the remainder of the team. "Hi! I'm Donna, your new assistant coach. I'll be working with Nancy to help you girls hone your softball skills. We're going to start with a lap around the field to get your muscles warmed up."

The entire team groaned at the thought of running, threw their gloves on the field and all followed each other slowly jogging around the perimeter of the large field.

Nancy walked next to Donna. "Wow. Do you possess magic? How did you get them to do that? I've been asking them to do it for weeks and they always just slowly walked it and maybe jogged a couple steps at best."

Donna shrugged. "I guess I didn't give them a choice. Sometimes you have to be a bit of drill sergeant at practices."

Nancy smiled. "I'm impressed. I think I'll learn a thing or two from you myself. You know, I never played softball. I was a soccer player. The school couldn't find anyone to coach the softball team, and they were desperate, so I took it on. I love doing it, but I'm so glad you're here."

Donna grabbed a loose ball and tossed it up in the sky and caught it, then yelled out to the girls who were finishing up their lap. "Ok everyone, meet me in the middle of the field for introductions and to get ready for our next warm up. I don't want to see anyone walking either. Jog right in."

The girls were huffing and puffing as they jogged in to meet Donna near the pitcher's mound, stopping to bend over with their hands on their knees to catch their breath.

"So, like I said, I'm Donna and I'm your new assistant soft-ball coach. I used to play softball here many moons ago. In fact, I was inducted into the hall of fame here for softball. You can see my name on a banner still hanging in the school gym. Now, besides that, I know a thing or two about being a good softball player. I notice you girls need some work on that. Can everyone in the group go around and introduce yourself and tell us a little something about yourself."

After introductions, the girls started chatting with each other, which started to get out of control.

Donna grabbed the whistle out of her pocket that she'd secretly kept stashed away just for this reason and sounded it off.

The girls immediately stopped talking.

"OK. You five,"—Donna pointed to a group of girls— "wait by the pitching mound, and I want the rest of you to grab your gloves for a batting and fielding drill. Snap to it! Whoever doesn't jog to the bats or gloves has to run another lap, and don't think I'm joking."

Nancy chuckled. "You heard Coach Donna. Let's put some real effort into this practice!"

The girls groaned again, but every one of them jogged to their positions, already a difference from earlier in the day.

Nancy put her sunglasses on and scooped up a few stray balls. "Do you want me to pitch to the girls?"

Donna shook her head. "I forgot to tell you. I'm in the Hall of Fame for pitching. I need a little warming up, so I'll handle the pitching if you want to take that group into the outfield and run some hitting drills—make sure the girls are swinging properly. I'll keep an eye on the infielders."

Nancy smiled. "Perfect. You know, I have a really good feeling about this fall ball season. By the way, is the reselling business still doing good? You're finding good stuff at the thrift store?"

Donna laughed. "It's going amazing. I can't thank you enough for the opportunities you have brought my way. I made in a week last week what I made in a month at my old job in California. I've actually started secretly looking at places to live. I didn't want to tell anyone just yet, as I don't want to jinx anything, but I can't stay at my parents forever and the business is already taking over their basement. I need *lots* more room."

* * *

Across town, Sarah finished her shift at the coffeehouse at 8 p.m., and made her way to her car, apron in hand. She opened the door and slumped into the driver's seat, then adjusted the mirror to look at herself.

"This is it, Sarah. You have to be able to communicate with Chris if this is going to work. Just talk to him about your concerns with the messiness," Sarah said into the mirror.

She sighed and shifted the car into drive, turning up her favorite song, which just so happened to be on the radio at that moment. She drove to Chris's house, or their house now as it seemed.

She turned the car off and sat for a few minutes, trying to decide how to go about the whole situation when she suddenly heard a loud knock on the window that jolted her. She looked over to see Chris smiling.

"Hey, you. You've been sitting there for a while. You plan on coming in?" Chris asked.

Sarah got out of the car and smiled. "Yes, of course. I was just … thinking. There's been some stuff on my mind lately."

Chris furrowed his brow. "Really? Like what?"

Sarah leaned down to pick a tissue up off the sidewalk that had somehow found its way out of the house with Chris. "Well, *this* actually."

Chris chuckled. "A tissue? That's what you're thinking about?"

Sarah rolled her eyes. "Chris, it's not just this tissue. It's the twenty or so used ones that I find all over the house in places they shouldn't be. It's gross."

Chris grabbed the tissue from her, embarrassment plain on

his face, and tried to laugh it off. "This is something I can definitely change."

Sarah sighed. "It's not just the tissues, Chris. It's the dirty laundry everywhere. It's the old moldy food that sits in the fridge forever. I can't live like this. I guess I never realized it until now, but I'm somewhat of a neat freak, and you, I've come to find out, are not. We need to—"

Before Sarah could finish, Chris hung his head in shame and embarrassment. "I didn't know you felt this way. I guess I didn't realize I was even like this. These last years of living alone have really made me loosen up and care less, I guess. What can I say? I'm mortified that I haven't noticed."

Sarah rubbed the back of her neck not sure of what to say next. "Look, I care a lot about you, Chris. I just—"

Chris cut in. "Stop right there. I need to go be by myself for a bit to collect my thoughts. I'm going to go take a drive. I won't be too long."

Sarah felt tears welling up in her eyes. She'd dreaded this conversation, and here it was … going terribly. Had Chris taken it as a personal attack? Would he even want to work these issues out with her?

Chris drove to his favorite spot near the ocean and walked down the beach a ways, looking up at the night sky in the process, until he came to a woman sitting by herself looking out towards the ocean.

"Margaret?" Chris asked, bewildered to see her sitting alone.

"Chris?" Margaret asked, just as surprised to see him there.

"What are you doing here?" Chris asked while looking out at the ocean where Margaret was looking, but not seeing anything.

Margaret took a deep breath. "I come out here to think sometimes. I need my alone time, not to mention, getting on the beach every day is part of the pact I made this summer with my sister. You?"

Chris looked back at the beach he'd just walked down. "I guess you could say I'm doing the same thing. Just getting some alone time to think."

Margaret nodded. "Want to talk about it?"

Chris felt his heart leap for a second as he sat next to Margaret on the sand. "Actually, yeah. Sarah just told me something that kind of ripped my heart out."

Margaret looked out towards the ocean. "I'm going to go out on a limb and assume that she talked to you about being less messy?"

Chris groaned. "She told you? I'm mortified even more."

Margaret put her hand on Chris's shoulder. "Don't be. Women tend to open up to each other more than men do sometimes. We are like each other's therapists. Yes, I know about it, but I also know she's been trying to figure out a gentle way to talk to you about it. She doesn't want to hurt you or screw up the good thing you two have, but it is something she wants you two to work on."

Chris took a long, deep breath, then formed a little smile while looking over at Margaret. "So, she thinks we have a good thing, eh?"

Margaret laughed. "Yes! Don't you?"

Chris laughed. "Heck yeah. I guess I just liked hearing it said out loud. You wonder how someone really feels about you sometimes, you know?"

Margaret looked back towards the water, this time catching a glimpse of the mystery woman heading out for her swim. Chris happened to see her too.

"Wait a minute. Is that woman going into the ocean in the middle of the night? Alone? Without any lifeguards or people around?" Chris asked shocked.

Margaret nodded. "Yep. I think she does it every night. Up until now, she's been my little secret. I'm completely interested in why she does this and who she is. I've been coming out here to think, but find myself coming to this same spot to watch her swim. I almost feel like I'm here to make sure she's safe. It's weird."

Chris stared in disbelief at the woman as she dove headfirst into a wave. "This is crazy. Doesn't she know that it's dangerous? Can't she join a local pool and get her swimming fix in that way? I have so many questions."

Margaret laughed. "Me too, Chris. Me too."

Chris stayed and watched the woman swim for a bit next to Margaret, then he stood up and brushed the sand off of himself.

"Well, I guess I should head back. Sarah is waiting for me. What do I do to remedy this situation?" Chris asked, nervousness setting in.

Margaret wrapped her arms around her knees and sighed. "Do you love her?"

Chris crossed his arms, seriousness overcoming his face. "Yes, I do."

Margaret looked out at the ocean. "Then, you know what to do. Come up with a plan that appeases both of you. It's about compromise. Relationships take work."

Chris smiled and reached his fist towards Margaret for a fist bump.

"Just one thing. Keep this mystery woman swimmer a secret. I don't want to tell anyone yet. It's somewhat therapeutic. She inspires me. On that note, I'll walk back with you. Dave is also waiting for me with the girls who are probably kicking his butt at Uno right now," Margaret said with a chuckle as she stood up next to Chris.

They walked together on the beach towards their cars in silence, then Chris suddenly turned to Margaret. "You know, I do have to correct you about one thing."

Margaret scratched her chin. "What's that?"

Chris smiled. "Us guys *do* indeed talk to each other. Maybe not as in-depth as you ladies, but we do talk," he said with a wink.

Margaret laughed. "Oh yeah? Anything you want to tell me?"

Chris walked ahead of her, reaching the walkway off the beach first. "Oh, no way. I'm not saying a word. Not. A. Word."

Margaret shrugged. "Well, suit yourself. Good luck over there."

CHAPTER TEN

Judy, Bob, and the rest of the extended family that stayed arrived in the early afternoon at their campsite on the beach in Assateague Island the next day.

"Isn't this just wonderful?" Judy said as she stepped onto the beach where their campsite was located and took a deep breath of the warm salty air.

Mike walked out on the sand and dropped their tent and belongings. "Well, you can't beat this. Oceanfront camping views."

Debbie and Carol helped each other get their belongings in the tents that Phil and Jack had already set up before helping Bob and Mike finish theirs.

Phil swatted at the air. "These mosquitos are insane. Hopefully, the fire pit will ward them off as well as the insect repellant."

Jack sighed. "Here's hoping."

The sun burst out from behind a cloud and shone directly on them while anchoring the tents in the sand.

Linda stood up and looked around. "Are we going to fry in these tents? There's not a lick of shade out here."

Bob nodded. "Well, that's beach camping for you. No trees

on the beaches. Perhaps a rain tarp or canopy can help with that? I'm sure we'll be off somewhere during the hottest part of the day anyway."

"Is everyone finished setting up? Anyone hungry?" Judy asked to the group.

"I definitely am," Mike said rubbing his stomach. The rest of the group agreed.

"Well, let's go into town and grab something to eat and then, we can come back and walk some of the trails," Judy said as she started off to the car.

After a hearty meal at a local place, the group made their way back to Assateague Island, setting off on foot down one of the many trails.

A handful of wild horses grazed ten feet away as the group walked down a man-made boardwalk trail bordered by trees and bushes.

"I can't believe it. Wild horses. I've never seen them before," Debbie said, pointing.

The ladies pulled out their phones to take photos with their mouths dropping open. The horses didn't seem to care about their presence, clearly used to seeing humans at this point.

Linda inched closer to one of the horses.

Bob yelled out, "Linda, don't go near them. They're wild, and we aren't supposed to approach them per the rangers. They are known to bite or kick, which is dangerous."

Linda retreated to view the horses from a safer distance, this time smacking at hundreds of mosquitos that swarmed over her. "Are you all getting eaten alive like I am right now?"

Everyone else started smacking their arms and legs, trying to get the bugs off of them. "Yes!" they chorused.

Another family walked by in full pants and long-sleeved shirts and chuckled. "If you're going to be out here, you're going to get eaten unless you wear long sleeves and pants, and even high socks. These bugs are the worst we've ever dealt with. No amount of bug spray keeps them away. We camp here every year. Just wait until nightfall."

Debbie widened her eyes. "Nightfall? And you all still come here every year with this issue?"

The man from the family responded, "Well, we've found ways to still enjoy being here without all of the hassle from the bugs. For one, we stay in our camper now instead of the tent. Are you all camping on the beach?"

Carol sighed. "Yes, but getting less excited about it by the minute."

The man chuckled again as his family walked ahead. "Well, it's a wonderful place. We love it here, but there are some things that you have to be prepared for, like the bugs, and the cold showers."

Judy's mouth dropped open. "Cold showers? No hot water?"

"Yep, you heard that correctly. You'll learn to take showers very quickly here," the man said with another chuckle.

Judy looked at Bob shaking her head. "This was your idea, Bob."

Bob shrugged. "Hey, camping was never meant to be luxurious. Everyone knows that."

After bidding their adieus to the family and finishing their trail, the family decided to head back into the seaside town to do some shopping, which there was plenty of.

Once they were done shopping, dinnertime approached, and Bob made an announcement. "Now, since we're camping, we're going to be making customary camping food for dinner. It's going to be delicious," Bob said, feeling excited.

Only Phil and Mike outwardly shared his excitement. The rest of the group sort of moaned, knowing it meant battling bugs once more.

Bob smiled. "How about the guys help me make supper, and you ladies can do whatever you want?"

The ladies nodded, feeling a little better about the men leading mealtime now.

Back at the campsite, the men got the fire going, while the ladies set up chairs for eating and hanging out, then set off on foot down near the water. The sun was setting and small groups of horses were walking in either direction near them on the beach, seemingly enjoying their beach walks as well.

By the time the gals got back to the campsite, it was getting dark out, and the full moon had gone up into the sky.

On the campfire, a large pot of chili bubbled away and some cast-iron skillets full of cornbread smelled divine.

"This looks and smells amazing. You guys did all of this?" Linda said eyeing the chili.

Mike nodded. "Well, Bob had all of the ingredients. We just really helped him chop and mix it up. I can't wait to eat it, I'm starving."

They eventually all sat around the fire, eating their meal, when a small herd of horses also noticed the food and came closer to investigate. Some, made their way close to the fire. Everyone stood up and backed away, but Debbie screamed.

"That horse is walking right into my tent. I never zipped it up after we came back from the walk. He's going to crush my items and get sand everywhere," Debbie said.

"Shoo! Shoo!" Mike said as he walked towards the tent.

The horse looked completely unfazed by Mike, but backed out of the tent, nonetheless.

After that debacle, they all sat down with their meals again, but this time the wind on the beach had picked up, blowing sand in every direction, including into their faces.

Linda threw her full-of-sand chili onto the ground. "I can't take this anymore. The bugs, the wind, the cold showers, the horses inviting themselves into our tents."

Bob shook his head and yelled out over the howling wind to the family members who all pulled their hoods over their heads and scrambled to get into their tents and away from the wind and bugs. "I'm sorry everybody. It seemed like the perfect camping spot."

While Bob was alone in the wind by the fire, and everyone else had scampered off into their tents, seemingly calling it a night and falling asleep, he closed his eyes for a minute, then heard a noise to his left.

"Woof!"

Bob opened his eyes to see an older scruffy dog—skinny enough so its ribs showed—snuggling up to him for warmth and licking its lips, probably from the smell of the chili.

"Hi, there. Where did you come from? Are you lost?" Bob said, examining the dog.

The dog barked again, this time nuzzling in closer as if wanting away from the wind.

Bob noticed how dirty and malnourished the dog looked. "Well, if you're lost, you've been lost a while, and if you're not lost, whoever owns you is not taking care of you. I can't give this chili to you. It might make you sick. I'm sorry."

By now, the wind had stopped howling, the bugs had mostly disappeared, and the full moon shone brightly on the ocean's surface. The dog jumped into Bob's lap and licked his face.

Bob laughed hysterically, causing Judy to unzip the tent and look out.

"What is going on out there? Where did that dog come from?" Judy asked.

Bob shrugged. "He just showed up with the wind after you all went into the tents. He's completely malnourished. I think I should drive out and get some dog food."

Judy hesitated, but then her heart melted as she watched the dog lovingly lick Bob's face. "Well, OK. Maybe we can make a little bed for the dog next to the tent. Grab a leash and collar while you're out."

A big smile grew on Bob's face. He loved dogs, and maybe

it took one being blown in by the wind to finally get another one.

By the time he came back with the dog food, the entire family once again sat around the freshly stoked campfire, each happily petting the dog, who seemed to be the life of the party.

Linda poured some wine for Debbie and herself, laughing all the while. "This camping trip is going to be one of the most memorable things ever."

Phil sighed. "I'll say, but look how nice it is now. A full moon with a campfire right on the beach facing the ocean. Wild horses walking in the distance under the moonlight. To top it off, we're all together, enjoying each other's company, *and* the bugs are gone."

Debbie swatted a bug on her arm. "Well, most of them anyway, but I can definitely stick this out a couple more nights."

* * *

Over in Cape May, Dave finished up in the kitchen and walked out to the dinner table with beautifully plated food for Margaret, Harper, and Abby.

"This looks amazing, Dave. Why are you so good at making tacos?"

Dave smiled and darted into the kitchen to grab his dish. "Well, I guess I've had a lot of practice over the years."

Margaret let the steam of her plate waft over her face and inhaled the aromas. "So, what do we have this time? Home-made guacamole on the side, slices radishes, freshly grated cheese, and even some lime wedges to squeeze on top? You've outdone yourself."

Harper took a loud crunchy bite of her taco. "I love Dave's tacos. It's my favorite thing to eat for dinner."

Abby squeezed her lime over her taco. "Mine too."

Margaret cocked her head to the side. "Hey! I make food. Don't you like my meals?"

Harper sighed, then took another bite. "Yes, we like your food too, but if we had to choose one meal to eat every night, it'd be this one."

Dave sat down at the table with his plate of tacos and high-fived the girls.

Margaret giggled. "We are about to get in a taco throw-down, Dave."

Dave smiled, and his blue eyes sparkled from the dining room light, while his white T-shirt showed off every muscular curve in his arms. Margaret tingled all over, sort of like back before they had started dating when she saw him walking by at the wildlife refuge. Over a year later, and he still gave her butterflies.

"I must say, it's been really nice having you all stay here while your family has been in town. Any idea of when they're leaving?" Dave asked.

Margaret finished her last taco and took a sip of her tea. "Well, they're all camping at Assateague Island with my parents today and I think until the end of the week, so maybe then?"

Dave thought for a moment. "OK, I think that could work."

Margaret paused. "What could work?"

Dave scrambled to say something. "Oh, um with you all staying here. I have some projects I want to do after you head back to the house."

Margaret's heart sank a little. He said he liked having them there, but then made it seem like they were getting in the way of his schedule. So many mixed messages. The whole thing confused Margaret.

After dinner, the girls insisted on playing Scrabble, so Margaret took that as her cue—time for her nightly drive and solo walk on the beach.

The sky was dark though the moon was full, and the water was the quietest and gentlest she'd heard it in a while.

She walked a ways until she came upon the mystery swimmer again. She felt relief to see her again for some reason, and she wasn't sure why. There was something about the unknown that intrigued her—something about someone so fearless and brave that riveted her.

Margaret sat on the sand, crossed her legs, and closed her eyes, relaxing into a deep meditation. She opened her eyes minutes later, startled by the sound of a voice next to her.

"I know you've been watching me all of this time," the mystery woman said, soaking wet and drying herself off. "Mind if I sit next to you?"

"No, not at all. Please sit," Margaret said feeling herself overcome with different emotions.

"I'm Sue. And you are?"

Margaret shook her hand. "I'm Margaret. I apologize if I've creeped you out this whole time. I didn't realize you've seen me sitting here. I just find it so fascinating that someone would just swim alone in the ocean at night. Aren't you scared?"

Sue toweled off her gray hair, and laughed. "No. Of course not. There's nothing to be scared of. I was a champion swimmer in my day. I can handle that water. What I'm more scared of is this world we live in. Being out there in the ocean, I forget all the awful stuff going on and I become one with nature."

Margaret looked out at the water. "Well, I'm truly amazed. I could never do that. I'm too afraid of riptides carrying me away, and not a single soul around to save me."

Sue leaned back on the sand. "Well, I'm eighty-one years old, believe it or not. Swimming has kept me so agile and in shape. It gives me life. It makes me feel so free and young."

"But doesn't your family worry about you?"

Sue nodded. "They do, but they also know that I'm going

to do what I want regardless. They've accepted that. But enough about me, what about you? What makes you walk alone on this beach every night?"

Margaret laughed. "Well, I like to think, and being alone is something my soul craves sometimes."

Sue sat up and looked Margaret in the eyes. "Well, what are you thinking about?"

Margaret shrugged. "Just stuff. Life, I guess."

Sue studied the ocean. "Who is he?"

"'Who is he?'" Margaret asked back.

Sue looked back at Margaret. "Yes, who is *he*? What's his name?"

Margaret sighed and wrapped her arms around her legs as a cool breeze blew through. "Dave."

"And why do you come out here to think about him?" Sue asked, seemingly reading Margaret's mind.

Margaret sighed. "You're good. You know that?"

Sue smiled. "Hon, I've got a lot of life experience. I've been in your shoes."

Margaret turned serious again, looking down the beach this time. "We're in love, well at least I think we are. He just bought a house right on the beach here. I have my own home still in West Cape May. Everything is picture-perfect except for one thing that really nags at me. He discusses his future as though I'm not in it. I'm divorced, and I don't have time to waste anymore, you know? I need to know now if this is *it.*"

Sue scratched her chin in thought. "Talk to him about the future that you see with him. Maybe he somehow thinks the same thing about you? Do you not discuss your future as though he's in it? Have you ever thought of that?"

Margaret thought for a moment. "Well, I never discuss it as though he's not in it, but I've never brought up buying a house together or even …"

Sue bit her lip. "So, you've never discussed how you both

feel about getting married again someday? It's never once been brought up?"

Margaret shook her head. "Nope. We both went through painful divorces. Honestly, marriage again seems scary, I think for the both of us."

"Would you say yes if he asked?" Sue asked.

Margaret leaned in and whispered over the wind to Sue.

Sue nodded and got up, brushing the sand off of herself. "Well, it was nice meeting you, Margaret. I have to get home to my boyfriend now."

"Boyfriend?" Margaret asked shocked.

Sue laughed. "What? An eighty-one-year-old can't have a boyfriend?"

"Oh, no, I didn't mean it like that. I guess I assumed you had a husband," Margaret said nervously.

Sue looked out at the sea. "I lost my husband of fifty years ten years ago. It's when I started swimming in the ocean by myself. It became a release for me. My boyfriend, Jim, found me the same way you did, while walking on the beach at night, wondering who the mystery woman in the water was."

Margaret smiled and stood up next to Sue. "Well, it was so nice meeting you, Sue. I hope you don't mind if I come out here to watch and think again in the future."

Sue smiled and started off towards the stairs. "I don't mind at all, but the next time I see you, I'm hoping you'll have some concrete future plans with Dave. Talk to him. Tell him your dreams and ambitions. Tell him what your heart desires. I think you may come out surprised in the end."

CHAPTER ELEVEN

Liz walked through the furniture store, taking note of different couches and lounge chairs that would work around the hotel. Melody tagged along, notebook in hand.

"So, why are we here? You know you can see this and much more online, right?" Melody asked as she slumped into a brown leather display couch.

Liz rolled her eyes on the inside as she sat in a cream-colored mid-century chaise lounge. "Because seeing and feeling these pieces in person is something you can't get online. Not to mention, the customer service here is top notch. They can answer most questions I have right away. What do you think of the couch you're sitting on?"

Melody leaned back even further into the couch, trying to get comfortable. "It's alright, I guess."

Just then, an outgoing guy with thick, black-rimmed glasses came out from the back. "Liz! Oh my! I'm so glad to see you. What hip new project are you working on?"

"Stan!" Liz got up to give him a hug. "This is Melody. She's helping me."

Stan nodded hello to Melody.

Melody crossed her arms. "I'm not *helping* her. We're working together."

Stan grinned and rubbed his hands together in anticipation "Well, what can I do for you ladies? You should *see* what we have in the back. It's gorgeous."

Liz nodded while taking a peek through the tiny window on the back door to see what was there. "Well, we are doing the interior design for the new hotel in Cape May, The Sand Pit. Melody's uncle, Fred, is the owner."

Stan winked. "Oh, I see. Well, you know the drill. Tell me the aesthetic and what you're going for, and I'll show you what I think will work best. Then, we can go over measurements and all that to make sure it's the right fit."

Melody stood up next to Liz. "Well, I originally had a minimalist design, but my uncle hired Liz to change that. Personally, I liked what I did."

Liz widened her eyes at Stan. "She's correct. So, the outside has a tiki bar with sand everywhere, giving it a beach feel. It's very cool. Inside is a blank slate. Literally. What I'm thinking is a tiki retro style but also modern at the same time. Something that makes the guests feel nostalgic and at home, but also invokes feelings of being at the shore. Do you know what I'm getting at?"

Stan nodded and clapped his hands together. "Do I ever! Girl, I literally hand-picked items for our store exactly as you described," he said as he opened the back door to an enormous warehouse with two floors full of every type of furniture and decor style you could think of.

Melody's mouth dropped. "Woah. This is so ... neat. We never saw anything like this during college."

Liz smirked. "Well, I'm about to show you things they never taught you in college. On that note, I'm sure we will utilize your minimalist design in certain areas, so be at the ready for that."

Melody nodded, finally realizing that something educational and fantastic was about to come from working alongside Liz.

* * *

Dale and Donna sat at a little picnic table under an umbrella at a restaurant along the harbor with lots of boats docked.

The seagulls stood ten feet away on different dock posts staring at the food on people's plates and sometimes attempting an unsuccessful flyover to steal it.

A waitress brought their drinks, took their orders, and left. Meanwhile, Dale grabbed both of Donna's hands across the little table.

"So, we finally found a moment in our busy lives to see each other. It's been a whole week. What's up with that?" Dale asked.

Donna smiled and shrugged, then looked out towards the water. "Well, like you said, things have gotten busy in our lives. You have your restaurant and new boardwalk cart, and I'm running my reselling business and coaching softball now. On top of it all, we live an hour and a half apart. It's not that easy to swing by and see each other. That's three hours round trip."

Dale looked over at a boat that slowly pulled out of the harbor. "Yeah, about that …. I've actually been looking at houses around Cape May."

Donna cocked her head to the side, feeling herself grow excited. "Really? Why? That's one long commute to your restaurant."

Dale looked back at Donna. "Well, I'm happiest down here. I'm completely enamored with the shore and with you."

Donna blushed. "So, you're going to commute three hours a day to your restaurant in Collingswood?"

Dale shook his head. "No. Probably once or twice a week. I have an exceptional manager and assistant manager who can handle things just fine without me there. It would free me up to focus on other ventures like my funnel cake stand, among others I've been dreaming up."

Donna smiled. "Well, this is a happy surprise, but I do have something to admit myself. I've also been looking at places to live. I was thinking about putting an offer in on a small house around here."

Dale's eyes widened. "Really? Why are we like this? We both were doing the same thing and didn't even talk about it."

Donna shrugged. "I don't know. I figured moving here wasn't an option for you, so I didn't mention it. And I didn't have any desire to move anywhere else. I'm also completely enamored with my hometown, even all these years later."

Dale nodded. "Understandable. Well, I was getting ready to put an offer into a house. It's beautiful with lots of room."

Donna bit her lip. "Interesting. The house I'm looking at is just adorable. Quaint and cute."

Dale stuttered. "Well, uh, would … would you consider maybe looking at houses together?"

Donna smiled. "Dale, are you insinuating that we buy a house together?"

Dale smirked. "Too soon?"

Donna sighed dreamily as she gazed out at the water, this time thinking about what life would be like with Dale in a home together. "Hmm … hard to say. Why don't we drive by the houses we're interested in after we leave here. I'm a little partial to the house I found."

The waitress placed their meals in front of them, and Dale looked up and smiled at Donna. "That could work."

* * *

Sarah walked around Chris's house with a trash bag, throwing away any garbage laying around, while Chris squatted in front of the open fridge, tossing out all of the expired food. Sam made his bed, cleaned the toys up in his room, and vacuumed.

Chris's eyes widened at what he pulled out of the fridge. "These nasty, moldy strawberries are over a month old. They've been hidden all the way in the back this entire time. Gross. I'm so sorry I brought you into this home while I was living like this."

Sarah nodded. "Well, I'm so glad we finally had a heart-to-heart about it. Having a clean place to live is important. It creates peace within the mind, not to mention it's more sanitary."

Chris shook his head, disgusted with himself, and wiped out the empty shelves. "You know, why don't we spend the entire day fixing this place up?"

Sarah placed the footstool under the ceiling fan and dusted a thick layer of grit off the blades. "What do you mean? Clean it top to bottom?"

Chris smiled. "Well, not only that, but how about we start making this home just as much yours as mine. You have all of those framed paintings stacked in the back room. Let's hang them up. We could go to the local nursery and pick out pretty flowers for the front yard, and maybe stop at the home improvement store and pick some fresh paint colors for the walls. I'm ready for a serious change, and I want you to feel comfortable in our space."

Sarah smiled. "You know, I like that idea."

Chris stood up and looked out into the living room as Sam vacuumed it. "And you know, for the longest time, I've been wanting to rearrange the living room and get a new couch, a nice big sectional. Maybe we can stop at the furniture store too."

Sarah stepped off the footstool, wiping the sweat off of her forehead. "Are you sure? This is turning into an expensive day."

Chris put both arms around her and kissed her head. "Yes, I want this home to feel like *ours*, not just mine."

Sarah smiled and hugged Chris back. "I'm so glad we've

come to a mutual understanding over this. Relationships can be hard. But, if we're going to be painting and planting, maybe we should do this all weekend. I'm not sure we're going to get it all done in a day."

Chris smirked. "We have plans tomorrow that we can't miss."

Sarah cocked her head. "What's that?"

Chris chuckled. "You'll see."

* * *

Judy and Bob and the rest of the family returned from the camping trip happy to have had the experience, but certainly glad to be back in Cape May and sleeping in real beds.

Bob opened the back car door, allowing the stray dog to jump out. "There you go, Hugo boy. Go see your new home."

Judy smiled. "Hugo is going to the vet pronto. We need to get him checked out. I already scheduled an appointment with our old vet. It will be so weird being back there after all of these years of not having a dog."

Bob smiled, petting the happy dog's head. "Well, I never thought a camping trip would send me home with a dog, but here we are. Do you love him?"

Judy smiled while Hugo leaned against her leg for more pets. "Of course. He's ours now."

Bob smiled, and his heart grew two sizes, at least. He couldn't wait to take the dog around the beautiful walking trails of Cape May and even take him fishing and camping, not to mention lazy days at home on the couch. It felt like he'd received a new best friend.

Just then, Judy got a call on her phone. "Oh, it's Dave calling. I wonder what he wants," she said to her husband. Then to Dave, she answered, "Hi, Dave. We just got home from camping. Everything OK?"

Judy listened to what Dave said. "Oh. OK. Wow, how nice!

Really? So, you want me to keep the family around for another day? Oh sure, they would love that. This is spectacular, Dave. I'm so happy."

Bob furrowed his brow. "What was that all about?"

Judy smiled. "I'll tell you later. I have to call the rest of the family and let them know that they can't leave until Sunday at the earliest."

Jack and Carol walked in with their luggage since they were staying at Bob and Judy's house. "So, we're staying until Sunday now?"

Bob looked over at Judy who was talking away on the phone and shrugged. "That's what I hear. I haven't gotten the scoop yet, but I'm sure we will soon."

Judy briefly stopped talking and moved the phone off her face to look over at Jack and Carol. "Yes! It's important. You can't leave until after tomorrow."

* * *

Across town, Margaret stocked the farm stand with more produce and emptied the honor-system box of payments. There was about two-hundred dollars in there from the last few days. Sales had really picked up—everyone wanted their Jersey tomatoes.

She stood by herself, looking over the glorious farm. Nobody was home at Liz and Greg's house, the girls were with Paul, and Dave was busy working at Pinetree Wildlife Refuge. She had the entire place to herself for the first time in a long time.

Margaret walked around the farm, admiring how beautiful everything was. She stopped by the flower patch, leaning in to smell some of the fragrant, colorful flowers, when she noticed Dave's hat just sitting among them.

Margaret bent down and grabbed the hat, smiling from ear to ear at how happy this man made her. He'd been playing tag with the girls out here and could never figure out what happened to his hat. She put the hat on her head, immediately catching a faint whiff of his scent, and her body warmed. They weren't going to see each other until tomorrow, but maybe that would be a good time for her to inquire if his future plans included her and the girls. Sue had been right, she needed to discuss not only what he wanted, but what *she* wanted. It made her stomach knot, as she didn't want to chase Dave away—but they'd been dating a little over a year, it was time.

CHAPTER TWELVE

Greg stood at the entrance to his restaurant at 5 p.m. on Saturday. It was the official, grand opening to the public, and not only had the staff gone through more thorough training, but the lighting outside had been updated, per the recommendations of everyone at the soft opening. Greg felt ready.

Guests arrived one by one for their reservations and most eyed the eating areas on the beautiful porch or back patio. The humidity wasn't bad that day, making for some perfect alfresco dining and socializing.

Greg held the door open and greeted everyone who walked through, smiling ear to ear. After having the host take over, he walked to the kitchen to check on things. Chef Ron, Chef Mike, and the rest of the kitchen team had it running like a well-oiled machine. The hot, freshly baked bread steamed on the cutting block, just waiting to be scooped up into a basket with the butter for the tables. Greg released a deep sigh and let the tension relax from his shoulders.

Having abandoned his stand, the host walked quickly to him. "Greg, I have a table out back that wants to speak to you. I didn't seat them, they sat themselves."

Greg furrowed his brow. "Well, that's odd. OK. I'll be right out."

Once outside, Greg saw his entire family—including all of his siblings and their families, plus his parents—had commandeered the large table. A rush of elation zipped through him at seeing them all, especially since there had been so much passive turmoil between his siblings.

"My oh my, this is the most pleasant surprise," Greg said leaning over to hug and kiss them all.

Greg's oldest brother Dan smirked. "Yeah, Dad said he'd take us out of the will if we didn't come, so here we are."

Greg's dad, Ken, laughed. "Uh, I never said that. I said I would just cut your portions to a quarter. Big difference."

The entire family laughed loudly, causing a nearby table to stop and look over.

"Who set this all up? Did you, Mom and Dad?" Greg asked curiously.

His parents shook their heads. "Not us, though I wouldn't mind being able to say that we had."

Christy—Greg's younger brother Joey's wife—raised her hand. "Well, funny enough, Liz contacted me about it, and we had a long talk about everything and decided this would be a nice thing to do on your opening day."

Joey rolled his eyes at Greg. "Can you believe it's taken our wives this long to reconcile? How many years has it been of awkwardness?"

Dan chimed in. "Well, Liz was the one who took the first step towards patching things up, so she gets all of the credit."

Greg's mom, Bernadette, held her wine glass up. "OK, can we stop talking about that? I want to forget about it, and can I get something poured into my wine glass already?"

Greg laughed and grabbed her wine glass. "Sure, Mom. How about I bring a few bottles of red and white for you all?"

His family nodded at the suggestion, and Greg went to grab the wine bottles.

Chef Ron caught Greg's attention. "I think your wife is roaming around. I just saw her."

Greg sighed and chuckled. "What on earth is going on? First my family's surprise visit and now my wife is walking around the restaurant."

Greg had walked down into the wine cellar to grab the bottles and talk to the server that would be waiting on his family, when the bathroom door opened next to him, nearly catching him.

"Liz? What are you doing?" Greg asked bewildered.

"Greg, did you look out back yet?" Liz asked curiously.

Greg nodded and smiled. "Yes, I saw them. I heard you set it all up. Is that correct?"

Liz nodded. "Yep, and believe me, I swallowed a lot of pride to do that. You know how it's been between your brother's wives and I."

Greg sighed. "Oh, do I. Well, are you going to go outside and eat with them or what? Why are you in here?"

Liz shook her head. "Oh, no. I already ate with my family during the soft opening, it's their turn to be with you. I'm here to see what time you're planning to leave the restaurant tonight. You haven't answered any of my text messages or calls."

Greg looked around at the now busy room full of diners. "Well, it's opening day. I might not get home until the wee hours. It's kind of a big deal."

Liz bit her lip. "How about this. Just for tonight, can you leave early? There's something special that you have to be a part of, but I'm not allowed to tell you what it is."

Greg sighed. "I don't know. That's asking a lot, and you can't tell me?"

Just then, Frank, the manager, walked up and grabbed the wine bottles out of his arms. "Want me to take these to your family for you? I've got a corkscrew in my pocket. I can take care of it."

Greg smiled. "Thank you, Frank. By the way, this is my wife, Liz. Liz, this is Frank, my manager."

Liz furrowed her brow. "Frank, nice to meet you. Say, how would you feel about closing up the restaurant tonight without Greg here. Do you think it could work?"

Greg hesitated. "Liz, I don't know—"

Suddenly Greg was tapped on the shoulder by Chef Mike. "Hey, you left this in the kitchen earlier," Mike said as he handed Greg his phone.

Liz eyed the phone. "Well, that explains why you weren't answering my calls or texts."

"Back to your question, Liz. I'm totally fine with closing up tonight. I've managed other restaurants before this. It's no big deal," Frank said.

Chef Mike cleared his throat. "I'm also fine with helping close up tonight. Between the kitchen staff and the front-of-house staff, I think we've got this."

Greg sighed and looked at everyone standing around him. "Fine. If it makes my wife happy, then we'll make it work. Thanks, guys. I owe you."

Liz squealed and grabbed him for a big hug. "I'll pick you up around seven. We need to get there by eight."

Greg's eyes widened. "Seven?! That's prime dining hour. We'll be at our busiest."

Liz made a frown face.

Greg rolled his eyes. "Fine. But this better be worth it, and it can't happen all of the time. I've got a business to run."

Liz smiled, then started up the stairs. "Trust me, this is once-in-a-lifetime thing."

* * *

Over in Ocean City, Sarah helped Chris guide his pontoon boat around the other boats as they approached the dock. The boats looked festive, each fully decorated for the 70s music theme, festooned with multicolor string lights, and lit up in the bay.

"Margaret and her family will be here any minute. Are you sure we have enough room for everyone?" Liz asked, eyeing the length of the vessel.

Chris turned the engine off, letting the boat glide gently to a standstill at the dock. "Plenty of room. Remember, I use this for tours. Oh, look. Is that Judy with the family walking up?"

Judy smiled and waved. "Hi, Sarah! Hi, Chris! We're here. I'm so excited to partake in this year's Night in Venice," she said with a wink.

Sarah stood on the dock helping each of Margaret's family members board the boat. "Welcome. So, glad you all could make it. You've all met Chris on the beach the other day, right? This is his boat, and he'll be captaining us. It'll be great."

Aunt Linda pulled her visor closer to her eyes. "Night in Venice, eh? Sounds interesting. What's it all about?"

Sarah smiled and pointed at the many decorated boats floating in the bay. "It's like a boat parade with decorations and contests, then it finishes off with fireworks at the end. We're a little late, so we'll tag along at the back of the parade once Margaret gets here."

Liz and Greg, who had also just arrived, nodded in agreement with Sarah. "Aunt Linda, you're going to love it. It's such a special night," Liz said with a smile.

Moments later, Margaret came running up behind everyone with Abby and Harper in tow. "We're here! Harper couldn't find her Ocean City shirt, and you know that *had* to be located and worn before we arrived," Margaret said with a giggle and an eye roll.

Sarah gave Margaret a big hug. "My friend. I'm so excited to see you. Tonight is going to be great."

Margaret smiled and walked onto the boat. "Yeah, you know, I tried calling Dave a few times to see if he could make it after work, but I never heard back. He would love this."

Judy cut in. "Hon, maybe he'll call once he's out of work and can meet us here. Don't worry about it."

Debbie nudged Judy. "Yeah, don't worry about it."

Chris started up the engine. "OK, everyone, we're going to head out to the parade route. Relax and enjoy the sights and sounds. You'll notice tons of people will be watching from their docks and bayfront homes. It really is a lot of fun, and something everyone looks forwards to every year."

Sarah opened a large cooler in the back. "We've got every kind of drink you could want in here. Help yourself."

Everyone found a seat or stood at the front of the boat, watching and partaking in the fun event. The sun slowly set, and as the darkness crept in, the decorated lights from all the boats lit up the bay and sky in all different colors.

Chris turned down his music as another boat approached closely, just as the fireworks began going off.

Margaret was in the back getting something out of the cooler, when everyone in the boat looked back towards her. She turned around with her drink and a furrowed brow. "What? Why is everyone looking at me? Did I do something?"

Abby and Harper squealed. "Mom, get up front *now!*"

Margaret sighed. "One second, let me just find a paper towel."

The rest of the boat cackled. "You may want to listen to your daughters," Uncle Mike said with a smirk.

"Fine. Fine," Margaret said as she walked to the front of the boat and leaned her elbows on the railing. "What is it you want me to see?"

Just then a few large fireworks went off in the sky and Margaret looked over while leaning on the railing, letting the soft bay breeze blow through her hair.

The boat next to them inched closer, and a marching band on board starting playing loudly, this time causing Margaret to look. There, on the boat, stood Dave leaning over the railing staring and smiling at Margaret.

"Dave! What are you doing on that boat?" Margaret yelled over the music, completely shocked to see him.

Dave smiled, then after the band was finished playing, thanked them and stepped off the boat onto Chris's pontoon boat and made his way towards Margaret. Her family and friends all moved to form a path to her.

Margaret smiled. "This is crazy. What is going on? Why doesn't anyone else seem shocked by this?"

Dave stood before her and got down on one knee, pulling a ring box out of his pocket and opening it. "Margaret Ann Wilder, I'm kneeling here before you and your family and friends, asking you to be my wife. Will you marry me?"

Stunned, Margaret threw her hand over her mouth, tears welling up in her eyes.

Abby and Harper jumped up and down next to Dave. "Tell him yes, Mom! Tell him yes!"

Overcome by so many emotions, Margaret began to cry and laugh at the same time, hugging and kissing Dave, and gently saying yes in his ear over and over again.

Meanwhile, the fireworks banged and boomed behind them, lighting up the sky and water, while Margaret's friends and family all cheered and whooped.

Liz and Greg brought out a secret cooler, then poured and distributed glasses full of champagne for a celebratory toast.

Everyone held their glasses up as Dave and Margaret, with their arms around each other, faced their family and their future, together.

EPILOGUE

At the end of August, the gals were on the beach together when Liz said, "I can't believe we've stuck to our pact of getting on the beach every day this summer."

Margaret laughed. "There were a couple days where we literally stuck our toes in the sand for two minutes at 9 p.m., but it counted."

Liz nodded. "It sure did. Even two minutes on the beach at night is therapeutic. My therapist told me that."

Donna giggled. "OK, sure. Whatever you say."

Sarah sighed while looking out at the water. "I don't want the summer to end. I love fall with every fiber of my being, but I love summer too. Can't I have both?"

Margaret took a sip of her drink. "Well, you're forgetting about locals' summer in September. Technically, we have another month of summer after all of the seasonal visitors leave."

Liz dug her feet into the sand and nodded. "She's right. No more crowded beaches or boardwalks. It's easier to get restaurant reservations, and the extra beauty of it? It's still the same summer temperature, actually maybe even better. We finally get the place to ourselves as everyone heads home for the season."

Donna nodded. "Yep, it was like that in California too. Same thing."

Sarah looked over at how Margaret's diamond shined brightly on her finger in the sun. "So, how's it feel being engaged to Dave?"

Margaret looked at the ring, twirled it around her finger, then smiled. "It feels pretty amazing. I'd been so wrapped up in him 'not including me' in his future plans, and he had me in the plan all along."

Sarah smiled. "Yep, we knew he was going to propose. Chris and Dave actually discussed doing the proposal on his boat and Chris told me, under the condition I didn't say a word, of course. Chris got his friend's boat and the marching band involved, as well. It was a great joint effort."

Margaret sat up. "Why am I hearing all of this for the first time? Who got my family involved?"

Liz laughed. "Dave called Mom and told her not to let the family leave until after the Night in Venice. They all knew what he was going to do too."

Margaret's eyes widened. "Everyone knew? Even my girls? I'm so oblivious. I guess I was so excited and overcome with emotion that I forgot to ask how he planned everything out. I can't wait to get his side of the story."

Donna's mouth dropped. "You haven't asked him yet? I would have asked ten minutes after he proposed."

Margaret laughed. "Well, I did ask, but he must have glazed over it, because I didn't hear any of *these* details. Plus, we're looking to get married pretty soon, so we've been busy thinking about that instead."

Liz lowered her sunglasses and looked at Margaret. "Really? How soon?"

Margaret smiled and shrugged. "Possibly this fall. We both want a fall wedding and don't want to wait a year."

Donna almost choked on her drink. "As in a couple months? How are you going to pull that off so quick? Usually, venues are booked a year out."

Margaret looked at her ring and then at the ocean. "Well, we were thinking of something a little less traditional. You'll find out when we decide."

Liz nodded. "Well, I'm sure whatever you do, it will be spectacular."

Margaret smiled. "Well, enough about me, what about you all? How are things with you, Donna?"

Donna chuckled. "Well, the reselling business is great, the softball team I coach just started their games, and they've already won the first three. Then there's Dale. He wants to buy a house together."

Sarah leaned on the arm of her chair. "Really? Well, are you?"

Donna smiled and shrugged. "We've only been dating a short while, and I'm still mending myself during a divorce. I'm hesitant to do something so big so quick."

Sarah laughed. "Well, look at me and Chris. We moved in together quite quickly."

"And how's that going?" Donna asked.

Sarah shrugged. "Well, at first it was a little stressful, but he's changed his lazy ways. We also redecorated, painted, and bought some new furniture. It's nice because now it doesn't just feel like his place, it feels like our place. Everything else is wonderful. The Monarch Coffeehouse is getting a lot of business and repeat customers, and life feels pretty great. What about you, Liz?"

Liz rolled her eyes. "Well, I finished that design job over at The Sand Pit, and I'm glad it's done with. While the money was excellent, it was a lot of work, especially at first when I was going head-to-head with the owner's niece. We eventually made peace, though, and it all worked out nicely. Her and I even have plans to have a celebratory drink next week. I guess I could say we're friends now, but I'm glad to be back to doing homes with my normal clients. We will all have to meet outside at The Sand Pit so you can see what we did. I love it."

The ladies nodded.

"Definitely. Sounds like a plan, but how is Greg doing?" Margaret asked.

Liz smiled. "He's doing great. The restaurant is busy, and he even talks to his siblings again. I guess his brothers' wives and I have made amends too. I got them to all show up on opening night of the restaurant, even made him leave early to get on the boat for the proposal. Gosh, I can't believe that was over a month ago."

Just then, Donna got a text. She sighed and rolled her eyes.

"Who's that?" Sarah asked.

Donna shook her head. "Adam. He seems to think I'm his best friend or something. He keeps texting and calling lately."

Margaret's eyes widened. "Does that bother you?"

Donna shrugged. "I'm not sure. Adam wants to move back here, and he keeps asking me questions about it … and about me."

"Did you tell Adam about Dale?" Liz asked.

Donna nodded. "Yep. Funny enough, once I did that is when he started calling and texting more. I mean, I could block him, but why would I? We don't hate each other. I'd like to be friends with him if I could."

Liz bit her lip. "That's great. However, you should figure out his intentions and maybe be open with Dale about it. I know I'd like to know if I were him."

Donna looked off into the distance. "You're probably right. I just feel so torn about this house idea with Dale. I mean, I've been with Adam since high school, and now I finally feel like I'm getting to see a more independent side of myself these days. I'm finally making decisions for what's best for me and not me *and* someone else, ya know?"

Sarah took a sip of her drink. "Have you told Dale that? You probably should so you're on the same page."

Donna sighed. "Sort of. I guess I need to be clearer. Hopefully, he'll have some patience with me."

Margaret stood up out of her chair and brushed herself off. "Well, ladies, I have to go pick up the girls from Paul's. I'm taking them to play miniature golf per their request. Wanna come?"

Liz laughed while standing up. "Are you kidding me?"

Margaret's eyes widened. "What?"

Liz pointed to a tiny scar on her wrist. "Do you not remember the debacle we had playing miniature golf with our entire family before the Fourth of July fireworks? Uncle Phil kept losing, got annoyed, and tossed his club willy-nilly into the air. He didn't think twice about anyone being near it, but yours truly was. Hence, this scar on my wrist."

Margaret laughed. "How could I forget? Uncle Phil is such a sore loser."

Liz giggled and looked at her wrist. "Funny enough, it didn't hurt that much, but it did cause a scar. Remind me to never suggest board game night when he's over."

Sarah laughed. "Oh, I have family members exactly like your Uncle Phil. Maybe they should meet sometime."

Margaret folded her chair and picked up her beach bag. "Well, I look forward to when family comes to visit again. They're a crazy, loud bunch, but I love them."

* * *

Pick up **Book 6** in the Cape May Series**, Cape May Locals' Summer,** to follow Margaret, Liz, the rest of the familiar bunch, and some new characters.

. . .

Sign up for my newsletter to keep up with new releases at **https://subscribepage.com/v8g9l9**

Follow me on Facebook at **https://www. facebook.com/ClaudiaVanceBooks**

ABOUT THE AUTHOR

Claudia Vance is a writer of women's fiction and clean romance. She writes feel good reads that take you to places you'd like to visit with characters you'd want to get to know.

She lives with her boyfriend and 2 cats in a charming small town in New Jersey, not too far from the beautiful beach town of Cape May. She worked behind the scenes on tv shows and film sets for many years, and she's an avid gardener and nature lover.

Made in the USA
Las Vegas, NV
16 August 2021